The Fourth Tale of La Croix de Bois

An Unexplained Breeze

Andy Stonard

Copyright © 2024 Andy Stonard

All rights reserved.

Andy loves to write. He also loves listening to everyone's stories and tales and always has done. He lives in France with his wife Teresa.

In the past, he has worked in alcohol and drug treatment services and also in policy both in the UK and internationally. In that time he would regularly speak at conferences and meetings. Then in France as a gardener. In between this he tries to write.

He has written two books - 'A glass half full', on alcohol use and misuse and 'In search of the ancients' on his travels around England and Wales with a group of mates looking at neolithic sites and pondering what they were all about whilst enjoying the banter that only a group of men can conjure up.

The 'La Croix de Bois' series is his first foray into fiction.

La Croix de Bois

The village of La Croix de Bois is a commune of 1624 souls. It is located in the Cotes d'Armor in Brittany, France.

The village is nestled in a valley surrounded by woods on all four sides with a river flowing through the side of the valley and to the left of the village, which feeds a lake to the west.

La Croix de Bois thus has somewhat of a micro climate, which often makes for contradictory weather compared to the surrounding area. It is inevitably warmer. The mists and fog can linger longer but it is always less windy and the combination creates a floor covering of wild strawberries in any untended area.

People have lived here for thousands of years, sheltered in a valley with food in abundance in the waters and in the woods.

Some of the existing buildings date back to the 12th century and the centre of the village to the 15th and 16th Centuries, with a cobbled square. It is an undeniably pretty place. It both calms and lifts your soul as you enter it.

All these buildings have been adapted and changed over the years changing functions as shops (magasins), workshops (ateliers), homes (maisons) and of course bars.

The church even harks back to the time of the Templars, with its dirt floor. To gain access to the key to enter the church you simply have to knock on the door next to the church and the 'boy' or his wife will hand you the key. They call him 'boy' but he is at least 94. He could be older but there is no-one around who is older than him to confirm or deny that, apart from a couple of women in the old people's home whose memory of nearly 100 years has long since waned.

The rest of the village has grown around these buildings and now there is, like so many villages in the area, a new housing development of new houses to the east of the village as it has grown.

In the summer the population is swelled by tourists and Parisians visiting their second homes.

La Croix de Bois, is a laid back village……………………most of the time.

Chapter 1 - The Village of La Croix de Bois

On the surface, the village of La Croix de Bois is like so many villages in Brittany – tranquil and beautiful. It is steeped in history with some fine old buildings. There is always an abundance of flowers. To the passer by, to the tourist and to the traveller it would appear exactly like that.

On another level, just like any village, it hides its stories and sometimes its mysteries. In the case of La Croix de Bois, there are many mysteries. Sometimes, there are mysteries that I do not understand. At times, those mysteries have a habit of revealing themselves.

Mysteries demonstrate and expose our relationships and beliefs; our strengths and frailties; our accidents and endeavours. Yet in truth, there is something more that is hard to explain; hard to put one's finger on. I have lived in this village for many many years. Not as many as some, mind you, and from time to time, I have been at a loss to explain certain things.

People describe La Croix de Bois as magikal and as a paradise. But as we know anywhere that is a paradise is determined by its inhabitants and secondly by outside forces and circumstances, whether it is nature, politics, economics or anything else. I can only explain about the inhabitants and to allude to these other things because I often do not understand them myself.

Mysteries are often entangled with secrets. Sometimes secrets are secrets because no one bothers to tell you a secret, or a secret is forgotten over time. A secret hiding place that is forgotten for instance. A secret longing or a secret fear. A secret health problem is something many people keep.

Then there are other types of secrets. Secrets kept from innocent or prying eyes, secrets locked away, guilty secrets, wrong doing secrets, secrets kept secret in order not to hurt or to worry others with.

There are also secrets that I do not want to be told or to know about. And if I know such a secret then I am a firm believer in it being left unsaid. Better someone else discovers it rather than it come from my tongue.

How do these secrets become unlocked? Sometimes by sheer chance, bad luck or because someone blurts it out, or there is a more mysterious reason that is hard to fathom that can trigger a chain of events.

Unless? Unless you really have to unburden a secret for the better. But even then?

It is Spring. The Winter had seemed to have lingered longer than was welcome. In Brittany, sometimes the weather can deliver all four seasons in one day. After two delightfully warm summers and an Autumn that kept warm until December, the months of January, and February served up a cold, wet and dark dish of the day, that lasted the whole period. It made the most optimistic and weather hardy folks miserable on occasion. I have to admit to being one.

At the beginning of March, the clocks sprang forward and we

welcomed in the later light evenings. But the cold hung around for a few more weeks, like a hangover or cold that lingers.

Yet the rhythms and cycles of nature edged ever onwards, so now we are celebrating the late commencement of Spring and the sun is starting to have a more leading role.

All of a sudden, the buds are budding and the leaves are shouting 'I am here, I am back...its spring'. The fields and woods look lush and dense after the sparseness of winter. Villagers are emptying out their window boxes and are planting an array of new brightly coloured flowers and plants. It is the same in the gardens.

The birds are building their nests and there is a general sense of throwing off the winter months behaviours and garments. The morning greets you with a warmness on your face rather than catches your breath.

I think about our ancestors talking about spring cleaning their houses after the long winter months. We are no different today but with modern day tools – the karchers are bought out from under the stairs or the shed to power clean the patio and the paths and an array of electric gadgets clean the glass in the windows, doors and window frames are washed after being opened to the elements to give their rooms a 'good airing'.

Well the modern tools that are working and do not need to be repaired or thrown away and replaced that is, after months of neglect in sheds and barns or under tarpaulins in the garden.

Washing appears on the washing lines and garden furniture is removed from where it was stored over the winter months into the garden. There are villagers trying on their clothes that seem more snug than they did last summer.

There was even one particular villager, who swore blind that he had been a victim of crime.

'Some bastard has broken into my house and dumped a suitcase full of clothes that are not mine' Jean Paul complained, when he opened a suitcase that lay at the bottom of his wardrobe.

'Jean Paul, we had to suffer you wearing those last year' his friend Gerard laughed.

'I swear to god that I never had this yellow shirt and this,' he spat holding up a pair of red chino trousers.

'We thought you were going to attend a Gay Pride march in that outfit' Gerard laughed again.

Jean Paul's sartorial elegance, or lack of it was well known in the village. We had, unfortunately all had to suffer his fashion taste, on many an occasion.

There is a background noise of lawn mowers and strimmers cutting the grass and the sound of chainsaws cutting branches on trees One can only describe it as a hive of activity.

Farid Khallil, the bee keeper is busy with his bees. His vast array of hives across the village and beyond have survived another winter. A further three people have agreed to have his hives on their land. Farid escaped the war in Syria with his children and settled in La Croix de Bois. As Jean Paul, my good friend, would testify he is more than doing his best to save the planet with his keeping of bees, and the honey is wonderful.

Chapter 2 – The Breeze

A couple of days later, there arrived what I can only describe as a Breeze.

It was very hard to describe – there was a vague shift in the air. It was slow and floating, almost like a thin line of cloud that drifted gradually through the valley and the village. The air seemed to be charged with electricity. You could almost see it but not quite. It sounds strange but you could sense what the eye could not see.

I do not think many people noticed it, or if they did then they took little notice. It was a Breeze that you could vaguely feel on your face.

When it went past the bar, the dishwasher suddenly exploded with water, soaking Marcel the bar owner, who immediately blamed Maria for not putting the lid down properly. Maria fired back straight away with 'the bloody thing doesn't work until you put the lid down, stupid.'

We all knew that It was married bliss, whether at work or at home together.

A teenager fell off of his noisy moped. Then stood up looking a little bewildered as to why his tyres had just slid away underneath him.

'I wish Jean Paul had been here to see that' one of the old men in the bar shouted. Gerard laughed, as he and Jean Paul shared a daily moan for noisy mopeds in the village.

'And this time we didn't need to put cheese wire across the square' which was their favoured but never implemented way of dealing with kids on mopeds.

When it passed the butcher's shop, Handsome Claude the butcher standing behind his meat counter, suddenly he seemed even more impossibly good looking than he already was. One of the ladies waiting to be served had to lean against the counter to stop herself fainting as she gazed at him.

The Breeze continued, onto the Pharmacy. In the Pharmacy, Cristal Lamar, the Apothacrist, or in modern parlance, the pharmacist, noticed over the next five minutes that some of her 'patients' looked more than a little perplexed - Madam Lebeouf came in for some skin cream for a rash but it had somehow disappeared on her way to the pharmacy. Then Madeline Pertwee came in for cough medicine but could no longer cough. Cristal, already renowned for her healing skills, wondered whether her powers had suddenly increased somehow. Over the rest of the morning hardly anyone came in as everyone felt well.

When it came downstream, so to speak, Jean Paul was up a ladder re-fixing a roof tile for Linda, who was standing on the bottom rung so that the ladder was secure. The floating bolt of energy wafted through them, making Jean Paul wobble a little, which in turn, jolted Linda to drop her cigarette in order to hold onto the ladder. She looked up and for the first time since she had known Jean Paul, which was for a long time, noticed that he had a cute arse.

When he came down the ladder a little more cautiously after the wobble he looked at Linda and she looked at him and they kissed on the lips. It was a lingering kiss. Then they leaned back from one another. He looked at her.

'Do you fancy?'

'Yes' she replied before he had a chance to finish the sentence. 'This evening around 7.00. That would be lovely'.

'OK' he said somewhat bewildered and then stepped forward and kissed her on the lips again. Linda, then shaking slightly, bent down, retrieved her cigarette that lay on the ground where it had fallen.

She puffed on it a couple of times and this time, threw the cigarette down. She grabbed Jean Paul and pulled him inside her front door.

'A drink at 7 pm tonight is a long way off,' She started, 'I think you need to give me a little attention right now,' and kicked the door shut with her leg.

Albert Jules, better known as the Professor, noticed something was happening as he was sat with me on a bench by the lake - all I could see were ripples on the water and the reeds by the side of the lake gently swaying, which I took to be caused by the wind. I could however feel a surge of energy that washed through me.

The Professor sat motionless and stared long and hard and without turning his head he whispered to me, 'The special wind has come and is passing through the village. Can you sense it?'

'Yes' I heard myself replying.

And it was continuing.

It headed for the Gestapo house. The Gestapo house is owned by Janine and Arthur Barnes, a retired English couple. They hate it being called the Gestapo house. It is a fine old mansion that the Gestapo decided in 1940 that they would occupy, hence the name. Firstly, because it was the finest mansion in the village and secondly, it dominated the village crossroads. So whichever way you left the village you had to pass the fine old mansion. When the Germans left in 1944, it was always known as the Gestapo house by the locals.

Inside the Gestapo House, the breeze was to cause a most unexpected find. Janine was decorating and as the wave passed she scraped too hard on the old wallpaper and a great lump of old horsehair and plaster came off the wall to reveal the back of the storage cupboard that was behind the kitchen. It had been sealed up from the kitchen side. Inside was a beer stein. She took them both down and put them in the washing up bowl and started to carefully scrub them.

Further up the road, the wave or breeze or whatever it actually was blew across an abandoned shed causing one side of the rotten roof to slide off. As it did so, it caught one half of the old large door at the front, which fell down.

What it revealed inside the garage was an antique Bugatti Type 35 car – a very rare French classic car.

News quickly travelled around the village and it was under a day before retired Inspector Didier Lauren came to hear about it. He went instantly to the shed to look at it and could not believe his eyes. What were the chances that this was the very Bugatti Type 35 that had been stolen over a few years previously, in a complicated case that Didier had never solved?

Inspector Didier Lauren's clear up rate for serious crime had been exemplary. The stolen Bugatti, along with two murders, one a salesman in the nearby village of St Pierre and one in the woods outside of La Croix de Bois involving hunters, were the only major crimes that he had not solved in the last decade of being a serving law enforcement officer.

Unfortunately, the stolen Bugatti instantly reminded him of the unsolved mystery of who had left a sack of stolen jewellery, along with a note, outside the Gendarmerie where he had been stationed, a couple of years ago. That and some odd group called the red monks who he was sure had been dispersing money to the villagers of La Bois de Croix but no one had ever confessed to receiving any money nor where the money had been taken from.

Now, if I had not been sitting with the Professor at the time would I have taken more notice of events? We often hear people explain things and events away as 'god's will', 'fate', in the lap of the gods', even 'it happened for a reason'. I have probably dismissed all of those statements because I have always believed that things just happen. They happen not for a reason but we take hours and days trying to reason why they happened.

And now here I am, sitting and trying to reason why this Breeze happened? Why? Because this Breeze triggered consequences to each and everything that it passed through or by. Some of these consequences were to have huge implications. Not necessarily the dishwasher in the bar, but even the kid falling off his bike, led the Mayor to finally install speed bumps at either ends of the square as a result of this accident.

For some people, however, the breeze meant their lives would never be the same.

Chapter 3 – The evening after the breeze

We were sitting in the bar in the village square. When I say we – Jean Paul, Gerard and myself we had been joined by Arthur Barnes.

What I had not mentioned previously, was that Arthur and Janine had not known that their house was known as the Gestapo house when they bought it. Naturally of course, the previous owner and the Immoblier (the French estate agent) were careful not to ever mention it.

What amused us was that when the Mayor commissioned an artist to draw a series of posters that chartered the history of La Croix de Bois, she made us all proud. One of the posters was a beautifully accurate drawing of their mansion with a Gestapo officer standing outside and a swastika flag hanging on the building. Now every tourist or visitor to the village can see where the Gestapo house is, much to Arthur and Janine Barnes' chagrin.

'Here comes Thierry the Exorcist' Jean Paul said, spotting him on the other side of the road.

Why is he known as the Exorcist?' Arthur asked.

'Poor Thierry has a serious alcohol problem. Well, actually he's a chronic alcoholic. He has worked all his life as a barman. An occupation as a barman, and a liking for the drink is something that goes hand in hand', Jean Paul explained, 'and in Thierry's case, hand in hand isn't even close to the truth'.

'But why the exorcist?' Arthur asked again.

'Because when he used to start a new job in a new bar, all the spirits disappeared.' Jean Paul said.

'But he's been sober for the last two years, which is fantastic' Gerard joined in.

'Does he go to AA? How did he stop?' Arthur asked.

'He walked into the pharmacy two years ago for his usual tablets and Cristal Lamar told him that the medication was a waste of time as long as he drank and now it is time to stop and he did' Gerard continued.

'Just like that?'

'Yes, just like that', Gerard stated, 'mind you, he is now the scruffiest man in the village. To say that he was sartorially challenged is an understatement. Look at him, he wins hands down in any clothing tournament. Look at him. He runs you a very close second in dress sense Jean Paul?'

Arthur and Gerard turned and looked at him. Gerard opened his arms to exaggerate what he was looking at. He had a pair of trousers that would best be described as ankle swingers as they were so short. They had also been eaten by his arse, as a considerable part of them had disappeared between his buttocks as he was walking. Below the ankle swingers were a pair of bright orange socks, partly covered by a pair of crocs. He was also wearing a Hawaiian shirt.

'You could put that yellow shirt and red chino's on you just found and challenge him for La Croix de Bois worst dressed man,' Gerard laughed.

It was Janine Barnes' birthday and Arthur had bought us all a drink to celebrate. Unfortunately we were still waiting for the birthday girl to arrive. Jean Paul and Gerard were asking what Arthur Barnes was doing for Mrs Barnes aka Janine in the evening.

'Well' he started, 'I am going to cook a special meal for her.'

'What are you going to cook?'

'For the main course I am making Smoked Salmon Pate with vine peppercorns with a champagne and verjus reduction cream. For the main course it will be Magret de Canard, pommes dauphines, thyme, soy and plum sauce avec crispy sage'.

Before either of them could speak, Arthur carried on.

'And for dessert, it will be bavaroise de noix, confit de figue, flambee aux bas Armagnac'.

He sat back in his chair looking very satisfied and sipped at his glass of wine.

'Is that it?' Jean Paul replied.

'What would you do for Linda's birthday then Jean Paul, now you are dating her?' Gerard asked, turning to his friend.

'Well', Jean Paul started putting his beer down on the table.

'As you know, I'm not one for expansive and complicated cooking. I thought that I would place a strawberry, with a good dollop of chantilly cream balanced carefully on the end of my knob'.

That was a conversation stopper and it was also when Didier Lauren, the ex-inspector joined us. Linda also joined us and sat down next to Jean Paul after kissing him and then sat holding his hand, which was most perplexing for all of us to see. At the same moment, Janine Barnes also arrived.

Jean Paul's proposed birthday dinner for Linda was not mentioned.

Didier called Marcel over and ordered us all a round of drinks.

'I must ring my colleague tomorrow about the stolen Bugatti' Didier says. 'It was owned by a guy from St Pierre. If I remember rightly, his name was Eric Gautier.'

'I know Eric Gautier' Gerard replies,' We have known one another for years and it is definitely his car. I don't know him that well but enough to stop and chat when we do see one another. That Bugatti became the love of his life after his wife suddenly left him, seemingly for no reason. She just vanished.'

'What do you mean vanished?' Jean Paul asked.

'Vanished, just completely disappeared. Eric could not find her and no one who knew her, could contact her either'. Gerard explained.

'When was that?' Didier asked

'Oh years ago. Let me see – at least 10 years ago, if not longer'. Gerard answered. 'Eric had tried to find her but with no success, she had a couple of cousins who lived in Jersey but they had not seen her. He never reported her as missing. She had withdrawn money from their account over a few weeks, taken her clothes and left. No message, no warning. She just left the dog with him. It was all a huge mystery'. Gerard told the story.

'Some people joked about whether he had done her in. Eric had been pretty confused and depressed for the first few months. It was a nightmare for him'.

'I'm sure it was' Didier agreed.

Slowly over the next few years he put his life back together. The house was still in their joint names, so trying to sort out anything legal was a nightmare as she was not deceased as there was no record of her dying, there were no letters, nothing. She had left no forwarding address, there was nothing legal. He could not sell the house and had simply got on with his life. That was why he was so upset when the Bugatti was stolen'.

'What is his situation now?' Didier asked.

'Well to start with, he will be delighted that his beloved Bugatti has been found. But I have not seen him in a couple of years, so it is a good reason to contact him,' Gerard started and then suddenly clicked his fingers.

'It was 2011 when Beatrice left him!' Gerard said conclusively.

'Can we try and see him in the next few days?' Didier asked

'I'll ring him and find a time for him to come over. He is only in the village near here'.

'St Pierre', said Didier, 'yes I know it. It was not only where the car was stolen from but was also where the murder of Vincent Duvall took place in 2010. Only one of a few cases I never solved before I retired' ex Inspector Didier Lauren stated.

'What was the other case Didier' Jean Paul asked.

'The stolen Bugatti,' he replied, 'and all those incidents in this village.'

Chapter 4 – The village of St Pierre

If ever there was a village that was the exact opposite of La Croix de Bois, then St Pierre was it.

The buildings were solid stone, the front doors and windows were all nicely painted. It was neat. There was no litter, there was no mess. There seemed to be no people. On any given day to drive through it was like driving through an abandoned village.

It was the Marie Celeste of villages. The bar was now closed permanently and there was no longer a shop.

In a nutshell it was a very bland looking village. There were no flower boxes or trees along the street.

Jean Paul called the village boring rather than bland. His view was that while La Croix de Bois was soulful then St Pierre was soulless.

Whereas La Croix de Bois lay in a valley, St Pierre was situated on higher ground. It was not on top of a hill but you could see a long way in every direction when you were in St Pierre and it was surrounded by fields rather than woods.

So it was windy and seemed much more open to the elements than La Croix de Bois. It seemed colder when you travelled between the two villages. Indeed, as obsessive as Jean Paul was, he always looked at the temperature gauge on his car or anyone else's and always commented on it.

'Look, two degrees less than when we were in La Croix de Bois' he would exclaim.

The church at St Pierre was imposing. Not unlike many villages throughout the region, the church tended to dominate. It was on a hillock and you had to drive or walk around it in order to reach the other side of St Pierre.

In truth, it seemed to stand like a sentinel reminding people not to have too much fun or laughter beneath its spire. That doom and death and even a suspended purgatory still lay in wait for the unfaithful and the unbelievers. Even if you have faith, do not expect to get away with anything.

It was not a village for heathens and pagans, not for the Celts and certainly not Parisians. Of Parisians, there were none. Local estate agents would not even try to sell a Parisian a house in St Pierre, it was an utter waste of time.

It was strange. It was not as simple as stating that La Croix de Bois was good and St Pierre was bad. It was almost as if they were contrasted against one another, almost a counterfoil for one another. As Jean Paul again would claim – La Croix de Bois and St Pierre were the ying and yang of villages.

It was a strange thing but when you have the time to drive through the two villages, you will understand exactly what I, and others, say about the two villages.

Chapter 5 – The missing Bugatti

As agreed, Gerard found Eric Gautier's phone number and rang him.

'Eric, it's Gerard from down the road in La Croix de Bois. How are you doing?'

'Gerard, how lovely to hear from you. How's life?'

'All good with me – listen, I'll not beat about the bush. We think we might have found your old Bugatti.'

'You are joking?' Eric exclaimed

'Well, I don't want to get your hopes up but we have found an abandoned Bugatti, same colour as yours and the chances of there being two must be pretty slim, so I said I'd ring you so you could come down this evening and see if you can identify your long lost car.'

Gerard explained how it had been found and they agreed to meet up in the village, which they did and Didier joined them. Then they walked up to the shed. Eric froze when he saw the car and was in no doubt that it was his car. He walked around it and opened up the side vents to the engine and looked inside. He walked back to the cockpit and tried to push the pump to build the pressure but it was stiff.

They looked around this old but beautiful car. Eric said that he would talk with the owner of the motor garage in St Pierre to arrange how to have it towed back to the garage. The Bugatti would need work on it as it had been standing still for a number of years. The car would require some love and tenderness to tease it back to life.

'It's an historic motor car and famous racer.' Eric started to wax lyrically about it and stroked the wheel.

'Not much fun being a passenger. There is no windscreen on that side,' Gerard pointed out.

'That's the design. Just for the driver. It is built for racing but anyone with any money wanted to own one – this is a real classic car,' Eric espoused further.

So the mystery of the stolen car was becoming clearer. Eric was insistent on taking Gerard and Didier for a drink.

'Now we've found your lost car, maybe we can find the ex wife' Gerard laughed.

'I finally gave up looking for her about three years ago but she still haunts me. My life has been great in the last few years but it has been a nightmare with her disappearance. I look back now and try to understand what happened – was she kidnapped, did she commit suicide or is she living a new life somewhere? If she left because of me, then for years I turned over and over in my head what did I do wrong or what made her leave? I know she was hot headed and not the easiest of people but she stayed with me even when I was sick.'

'What I need to do now' Didier explained, 'is to report this to my colleagues so the case can be re-opened so to speak. Between us we need to trace the owner of the old shed and how the car ended up there'.

They left one another after a further hour of reminiscing.

Didier duly reported the discovery to his ex colleagues, who within a day were able to ascertain the whole set of events.

As it turned out, the owner of the shed was an old guy who had passed away in his 80's. He had no children but a nephew, who had inherited the old shed and very little else. The nephew had arranged with a friend to steal the Bugatti, which they had then hidden in his old Uncle's shed in 2016

The nephew and his mate had been caught breaking into a warehouse later that year. The arrest then opened a can of worms for them both as a series of other crimes and break ins had come to light. There were over twenty break ins and the selling of stolen goods. Even worse, one the break ins had gone wrong and ended in a serious assault on the occupant. Found guilty on all charges, they were sentenced and are still incarcerated in prison and had never been able to move the car.

Chapter 6 – The murder of Vincent Duval

Ex Inspector Didier Lauren sat down at his new home in the village, in his armchair by his log fire. The discovery of the stolen Bugatti had reminded him of the murder case in St Pierre.

It was the murder of a man in the village of St Pierre, the village next to La Croix de Bois. In 2010. The murder of Vincent Duval. Didier poured himself a glass of Samur Champigny and reflected on the case as he looked into the glowing wood on the fire.

Vincent Duval was a 48 year old man. He was a salesman. He had been poisoned and the murderer had never been found. The case was still open, when he had retired.

Vincent Duvall lived alone and was quite a loner. His ex-wife, they had separated in 2008, was living in Bordeaux at the time of the murder. She had a cast iron alibi as she was a qualified nurse and was on duty on the day of the murder. Although separated, she had been both visibly shocked and upset when Didier had gone to meet her as part of his investigation.

From everyone Inspector Didier Lauren had interviewed, Vincent Duval appeared well liked with his colleagues and clients. The neighbours said that he was quiet, kept himself to himself and never caused any problems. He was always personable when they saw one another but he never invited them in for a drink and was very polite but always declined an invitation to do likewise at their homes.

He had no history of mental illness or drinking or drugs, no debts. He had two brothers who both lived in Paris. They did not see one another very often but would speak on the telephone about once a month. As they both stated, Vincent seemed quite content. He would talk about work and his beloved football team Rennes. In a nutshell, there seemed to be no motive for his being poisoned.

Vincent Duvall was not in a steady relationship. Neighbours had a suspicion that he might have been seeing someone but they had never met nor seen him with anyone. He was away from home a great deal as a salesman and Didier had confirmed this with his employers and with receipts for hotels and meals in other French cities and towns.

For Didier, he had never had a case that was so empty of clues, evidence and leads.

Chapter 7 – A Revelation over dinner

Eric Gaultier had his beloved Bugatti collected from the dilapidated shed and taken to the garage in St Pierre, where the mechanic and Eric with love in their hearts cleaned and lubricated it back to life.

Then, two weeks later, Eric Gautier proudly drove it into the village square after arranging to take Didier and Gerard out for a 'thank you' meal.

They sat down and ordered a ricard.

'Now, as I said, all we've got to do is find your lost wife,' Gerard quipped.

Eric shrugged.

'Who knows where she is? We had not had a good year together before she left me – arguments and that kind of thing. There was a distance that developed between us. It had not helped with me being so ill for what seemed like months. I was even hospitalised for two weeks with complications following a nasty case of what was originally thought to be food poisoning'.

'Food poisoning?' Gerard repeated.

'Not a great time to be discussing food poisoning when we are about to eat but it was horrible and I was very ill with it. Took me another two months before I was properly back to normal.'

'Why so long?' Gerard asked, 'I mean you usually get the stomach cramps and the wild shits and it's over in 24 to 48 hours'.

'This wasn't the first time, I'd had some sort of illness off and on for about 6 months – like a flu really, couldn't seem to shake it off. Guess it was some sort of virus or something, I wasn't in the best of form in myself or with the missus'. Eric explained.

'Then the last time, it was much worse so the doctor ordered some tests. He could not understand what it was that I was suffering from. Then this was the most bizarre thing is that with all the blood tests and what have you, they thought it might be hemlock. I'd never heard of hemlock. They tested me because I had developed a slight tremor and was having breathing difficulties. Luckily one of the nurses had seen these symptoms before when she was working abroad and talked to the doctors,who treated me for possible water hemlock poisoning. Lucky really, because untreated it can cause muscle damage and kidney failure. Apparently, in strong doses, it can even kill you'.

'Good God' Gerard exclaimed, 'I never knew. How on earth did you end up eating hemlock?'

'I do not have a clue – I might not even have eaten it. It is a plant that is around in France and you can come into contact with it through the skin'.

Didier remained silent and the three of them looked at one another.

'Didn't that guy in St Pierre die of poisoning?' Gerard asked, turning to Didier.

Didier nodded, 'yes, Vincent Duvall was his name and he died from hemlock poisoning.'

'So it must be naturally growing in the village then?' Gerard asked

'Yes, I thought that too' Eric agreed, 'but I did not know who to talk to and by then I had recovered and never thought about it other than as coincidence.'

Didier put his glass down.

'I never knew this Eric. I am sorry to hear what happened to you.'

Didier's mind was spinning from hearing this. In trying to solve the murder of Vincent Duvall he had not encountered this type of poisoning before. He and his colleagues had never considered looking to see if there had been any evidence of other individuals' being poisoned in this way. It was all deeply disturbing. Not surprisingly, all three of them had lost their appetite, apologised to the waiter and instead had some coffee and a ricard and then left.

Chapter 8 – Reviewing the evidence

When Didier arrived home he went straight to his cellar, where he had a box, in which contained photocopies of many of the documents that related to the murder of Vincent Duval. He also had his own notes that he had kept in a notebook, the original, of which he had handed over to the Inspector who had taken over the case.

Didier had always kept copies of documents at his home. He was not supposed to but it was not uncommon for him to wake with a key question or thought about a case. It was no surprise to Didier that he lived alone and always had lived alone. He was absorbed with his cases, which left little room for socialising and certainly not romance. He had met women on occasions but they had all quickly recognised that they came a considerable second to his work and they never lasted long.

So his solitary life had always been acceptable to him in his pursuit of solving the crime. His fear was retirement and how he would fill the vacuum that this left. This case was a temporary reprise and he could feel the excitement that it gave him.

He placed the box on his dining table. Poured himself another ricard and read through all his notes, the autopsy report and the crime scene details. He had forgotten how many times that he had read them but this time he was looking at them in a different light.

Retiring from work was one thing but an unsolved case which he had pursued for a number of years was another thing. He was not obsessed but he had never been able to just switch off from this murder.

He smiled to himself – he was obsessed. Of course he was out there with someone with motive and method to do this. Now there was something new that he had found out. It could be nothing, or it could be a link. He had to find out more, not least to eliminate it.

Death through hemlock poisoning meant it had to be ingested in nearly all cases. You could not just brush up against a plant like that and die. Just as poor Eric Gaultier had thought, as did Didier and his colleagues when they were investigating the murder. They had taken expert advice and the advice was that most likely, Vincent Duvall had died through taking hemlock into his digestive system. So either he had committed suicide through a very unusual process, or someone had killed him and never been caught.

He picked up his mobile phone and rang Gerard.

'Gerard, I am sorry to phone you but I am deeply disturbed. Coincidence or what with Eric Gautier and Vincent Duvall? I hate coincidences. The murder in St Pierre back in 2010. He was poisoned and the toxicology report included traces of hemlock. I researched the history of hemlock poisoning. Hemlock can be mistaken for wild parsnip, wild carrots and even parsley. It is not uncommon in France. The coroner's report showed no skin rashes or irritation, so the poison was administered orally either through liquid or in food. His stomach contents showed that he had had a meal of a chicken casserole'.

'His last meal!' Gerard concluded.

'Yes, his very last meal on this earth.'

'But you do not have any witnesses nor suspects?' Gerard asked.

'A complete blank. He lived alone, did not seem to have any enemies, there was no girlfriend or boyfriend or wife or husband. Neighbours thought that he had a lover the year before but they never met or saw anyone and he was a salesman, so he was away quite a bit and kept odd times due to his travelling'.

He paused to sip his ricard.

'And now we discover that your friend Eric Gautier, was poisoned with hemlock. I would like to speak with him again. Do you think that he will mind?'

'No of course not. He had given up on ever finding the Bugatti. The Bugatti had been stolen. Vanished, just like his wife had vanished. Getting it back was a complete surprise.' Gerard said.

And so close to home. Not under his nose but very close in the next village. It must have opened up questions about his wife again,' Didier summed up.

'Without a doubt.' Gerard agreed.

'Thank you Gerard. Good bye,' and Didier put his mobile phone down and returned to his armchair with his ricard.

His mind was racing itself. He had felt a surge of adrenaline about the case. It was a feeling that he had not had since he had retired.

Chapter 9 - The Gestapo House

Janine and Arthur Barnes are both retired, another English couple who had moved to La Croix de Bois. Janine likes to paint and she manages to sell the odd canvas. She is a talented artist, whose work runs to pottery as well. Arthur, was an accountant, just like Giles Pertwee, who said he was but of course he was not, as you will recall from a previous tale. Arthur often wondered at what sort of accountant Giles was as he seemed to have only a rudimentary grasp of accounting

They live in a grand house on the road just outside the village square. It is a huge rambling house that they have lovingly restored, but such is its size that the renovation has never been completed.

It really is a magnificent house, however as you know, it is the house that the Germans occupied during the war, forever known by everyone as the Gestapo house.

An immensely annoying issue to them both and not helped by the fact that everyone gives directions to tourists and visitors that in order to arrive in La Croix de Bois, you turn right at the Gestapo house and to leave you turn left at the Gestapo house!

When you question anyone in the village as to who exactly was stationed at the house, then no-one can tell you definitively it was the Gestapo. It is the story that has been handed down over the years.

In truth however the house was never occupied by the Gestapo and no-one was ever tortured there. The Gestapo stayed there, fairly regularly. much to the annoyance and disgust of the local Commander, Wilhelm Brun who was stationed there for three years. The arrival of Gestapo officers upset everyone – they were unpleasant characters and were responsible for the arrest of local men. It upset Commander Wilhelm Brun.

He was a soldier who had the responsibility to try and keep the peace in an occupied country. He did not want to be in France, he wanted to be at home with his family. He did not want the war but here he was. He had heard stories about other parts of France but the Bretons were different, proud and fiercely independent. Historians would refer to them as leaning towards communism and many of them were first and foremost Breton and then secondly French.

In his view, if Germany was to remain in charge of Brittany and the whole of France then they had to find a way to not only win the war but to build a trust and that would take years. He seriously did not believe either was achievable, certainly not in Brittany. For some supporters of Vichy France, it might work but not in Brittany.

The commander was a good soldier but he had only five men to control the area. The majority of the army were based along the coast especially in the deep ports of Brest, L'Orient and St Nazaire, the big cities of Rennes and Nantes and along the Cherbourg peninsula through to St Malo.

He also held the belief that their occupation was simply wrong, though he never shared this view with anyone, not even his own family and certainly not with his five men nor other commanders, even when that very same sentiment was being expressed.

His strategy was for a peaceful coexistence between the locals and his meagre force. Berlin, of course, would not agree but they were not here. He had seen enough death and destruction already on his journey through to Brittany. Berlin was still gungho as it was yet to be bombed to pieces.

He had remembered seeing the haunted face of his father when he returned home briefly in 1916 during the First World War, after two years of non stop fighting and living in the trenches and the incessant shelling. His father had watched despairing at a young French man die horribly and slowly at the end of his bayonet in the Somme. It was a scene that never left him. It haunted him day and night. It is not something that politicians and warmongers ever seem to consider or experience themselves.

He had barely recognised his withdrawn and depressed Father. It was his last abiding memory of the man.

All around him he saw the human suffering, the stench of blood, guts and decay, the mud, the incessant fear. He was given leave but at home in Germany he was detached and withdrawn, barely able to hold a conversation with anyone in his village and he had left behind four able and fit men from the same village who would never return.

When he returned to the front, he had simply given up and for atonement he sat in a trench in Paschendale watching English troops literally drowning in the mud when a shell blew him into oblivion. He died instantaneously and the remnants of his body were scattered in the mud and debris of war. None of his body was ever recovered and it remains to this day in the farmland of

France.

That was the simple reason that his son, Herr Wilhem Brun was as much of a pacifist as he could be. As history repeated itself and poor working men died across Europe on the backs of nationalism and for men far richer than they would ever be, whose responsibility was to ensure peace rather than killing and the brutality of war. They were the kings and czars, the politicians, who never had to fire a gun.

So Commander Wilhelm Brun kept control and kept the peace, as best as he could. No one trusted him at first. Certainly not the local French inhabitants and his five young soldiers. All were distrustful of the Commander. The five soldiers could see that he did not embrace the Nazi philosophy as they had been taught to understand it. But over time he won everyone over. His approach of caution and conversation rather than swift retribution and confrontation instilled a peace of sorts and a begrudging acceptance on both sides.

Commander Wilhelm Brun knew who the hotheads and troublemakers were, who were in the resistance and who wanted nothing but to keep their heads down. The resistance had started attacks in Brittany in 1943. By early 1944, the activity in the area had intensified. It could not be more obvious that an invasion was on its way. He kept his own five troops close and safe. He reasoned with the local resistance leaders to operate carefully and out of sight. If they did not do this, then it would attract retribution that he would not be able to control from above.

To his mind he was not being disloyal but was putting the people of La Croix de Bois and his troops as safe as possible in the wake of inevitable battles ahead and the hardship and suffering that would come with that. The German nation could no longer hang on to the whole of Europe.

Wilhelm Brun was determined to try and keep safe everything he had been put in charge of. The beauty of La Croix de Bois as a special place had soaked into him as it had with every invader and traveller for five thousand years. It had to be preserved as much as he was able to.

When the order came to leave, there was a dilemma. He wanted to say goodbye properly to some of the local villagers but the American and British troops had successfully landed across the Cherbourg peninsula and were heading towards central Normandy and what was to become the nightmare of the fighting in the Bocage. As a consequence, everyone on both sides were edgy.

He went to see the Mayor, to inform him that they were leaving and to wish him luck. His orders were to retreat west towards the deep water ports where the submarines were based and to meet up with other troops to defend the rest of Brittany

But for the six of them, they knew that they were not going home. What was incredibly fortunate for Commander Wilhelm Brun and his 5 soldiers was that they were relocated to Lorient.

Commander Brun fully expected them to be sent to St Malo. St Malo had been under siege and in a relatively short time had been flattened by bombing and taken by Allied forces.

After keeping his five soldiers and himself safe for over three and half years, it took a mortar round to hit one of the two jeeps that they were travelling in killing two of them instantly and seriously injuring a third. The shrapnel had wounded the other two and Herr Brun also. Given the wretched state of them all in the jeep, they were still sent to Lorient to join the garrison there.

Of his five beloved soldiers, who were like his sons to him, who he had promised he would get them home safe, two were now dead and a third one had lost a leg. The oldest was 23 and the others 19 and 20. All of them teenagers when they had first entered the army.

He had tried so hard to keep everyone safe. Whenever he was informed that the Gestapo were due to arrive he had everyone on best behaviour from his own troops, to the bar and restaurant staff to the Mayor, who informed the resistance through their networks, so they kept their heads down while the Officers were staying.

With no attacks or ambushes in the area, the Gestapo were happy with the Commander's reports. To keep their visits as short as possible and to hasten them on their way he helped the village to develop a reputation for poor food. Oysters that were off gave two officers violent stomach cramps. He made sure that the steaks were as tough as old boots and that the replacement steaks when the Officers demanded better steaks were even worse. The potatoes were especially selected with a nasty black tinge to them.

Naturally the best wine was kept hidden. Instead they would drink plenty of the cheap wine. That coupled with inedible food had worked wonders in encouraging short stay.

Thus the so-called Gestapo house was never occupied by the Gestapo but Janine and Arthur had to tolerate its nickname.

The slog through Brittany cost the Americans 10,000 fatalities, many in trying to capture Brest, which they had reduced to rubble.

To save time and the lives of more American soldiers, they had simply encircled St Nazaire and Lorient and left the German garrisons there until they surrendered at the end of the war.

Chapter 10 - Back to St Pierre

Eric was more than happy to see both Gerard and Didier again. If anyone could shine a light on Beatrice's disappearance, they would always be welcome. The three of them sat in Eric's kitchen.

'So tell me again Eric, when did your wife leave you?' Didier asked

'It was the second of January. We had a very quiet and to be honest depressing Christmas, and went to a party in the village on new years eve, where we hardly spoke to one another. On New years day we again hardly spoke. The next day, I went to work and when I came home she had simply gone. Vanished into thin air'.

'And you never knew where?' Didier asked

'Not a clue. Her car was gone, some clothes had gone, but not many. After a few days, I went through her remaining belongings, to try to find any clues. She had left her bank and credit cards, but took her other official documents. I was worried but given how we were getting on – sorry we were not getting on. I never reported her missing as it wasn't as if she had been kidnapped. After a week, I asked around if anyone had seen her. I took a call from her work a few days after she had left as she had not shown up there either.'

'Then what did you do?' Didier asked further.

'To my shame – nothing. As rubbish as our relationship had become, I felt empty without her. I missed her. I guess I became rather depressed and every time my phone rang or the postman came to the door, I hoped it was her'.

'But it never was' Gerard stated

'No, it never was. I eventually went to the doctor who prescribed me some antidepressants because I was so low, ' Eric admitted and then continued, 'after about six months I stopped waiting for the phone to ring or a letter. She had a sister in Angers. They had never been close and had not spoken to one another for years after they had some family argument. I drove to see her to tell her what had happened but she had not heard from her either. It was all a complete blank'.

'You read about these things but you never expect it to happen to someone you know and especially yourself. I thought I knew her but clearly I did not. I decided that I had to stop taking the medication and try to get on with my life. It sounds pathetic but when I found the old and rusting old Bugatti and bought it, I found trying to restore it really helped. It gave me a challenge.'

As Eric was talking, Didier was the maths in his head. The murder had taken place on the 12th December 2010 and his wife had left him on the 2nd January 2011 the day they both returned to work after the new year.

'I was also aware that there were rumours and gossip doing the rounds in St Pierre as to whether I had done her in and where I might have disposed of her body. Not one person in the village knew where she was and of course any interest in her disappearance faded completely as the police investigated the murder of Vincent Duvall. Why bother about a simple domestic break up when there was the possibility of a murderer stalking the village?' Eric concluded.

Didier nodded at Eric but did not pursue this summary. Didier had explained to Gerard before they had gone to see Eric that he did not want to go over the poisoning issue in case it alarmed Eric. It had alarmed himself and Gerard. Now he had a good grasp of the time lines, talking with Eric had done that. Now where and how to proceed?

Chapter 11 - Professor Albert Jules

Giles and Madeline Pertwee, another English couple who had retired to a rural lifestyle in the village, came and joined me at the bar. I always looked forward to my little interactions with them both. They are who they are in our lovely little village, but their pasts were very different. Did that matter? In a village like La Croix de Bois, you took people on face value and accepted what anyone told you about themselves, or did not tell you.

I enjoyed their company and their stories but it would be a great understatement to say they were involved in some of the escapades that had happened in the village. Without them and who they knew, some things would have turned out very differently.

Sitting opposite me at an outside table, they were looking a little awkward and in the end Madeline elbowed Giles and said 'go on Giles show him'.

With that encouragement, Giles coughed and bent down and pulled out three photos that were in his rucksack. They were photos of La Croix de Bois, which they had printed off.

'We wanted to show you these - the friend who sent them to us said that they were circa 1930. I looked at them and Madeline pointed out how the butchers shop and one of the restaurants looked so different today and then Giles pointed to a man outside what looked like a shop that sold hats'.

He passed the photographs across the table to me. 'Doesn't that guy there look just like the old guy in the village who is always walking? What's his name? The Professor? Can't remember his proper name' Giles stated.

'Albert Jules' I said.

As I stared at the photo I had to confess that it didn't just look like him, it was almost an exact image of him but for some reason I chose not to say anything to them other than 'it does a bit doesn't it?' to hide my surprise.'

We sat there enjoying our drink and talking about the changes to the village and I told them that there was a Facebook page dedicated to the village and its history. Of course, Madeline and Giles knew this, just like they seemed to know everything that went on in the village and further afield. They were never afraid to google anyone or anything they wanted to know. They always asked direct questions.

Jean Paul was convinced that they kept a file on everyone and everything. Their insight into global conflicts and current affairs always seemed to be incredibly well informed. I think Jean Paul was correct. I knew who and what they had been but they were never sure whether I knew. I liked to keep it that way

So it was even more intriguing three evenings later, when Jean Paul, Linda and I joined Gerard outside the bar on a lovely sunny evening, with the sun just fading over the rooftops. Jean Paul and Linda are now seemingly inseparable. Gerard was looking very serious.

Jean Paul ordered us all drinks and looked at Gerard.

'What's up with you this evening? You're very quiet'. He said.

Gerard looked at us both.

'I have just come from having a coffee with Pascal and Rose at their boulangerie, as they were closed between three and four this afternoon and they were showing me some framed photos that Pascal's mother had. They had removed a load of photographs from her house when they were clearing it after she passed away about three months ago. Gerard explained.

'The usual stuff of the people and the village and some of the old buildings but really old. A couple of them must have been from the 1890's or 1910 - or something like that. Anyway, one of them was a wedding group - there must have been at least thirty people in this photo. All ages, men and women and there on one side was the Professor, I kid you not. He looked a little younger but not by much'.

'It must have been a relative' Jean Paul suggested.

'I thought that' Gerard replied but when I turned it over, someone had written down every name of the people in the photo like you see on football teams and the like'.

'And?' Jean Paul asked.

'And there on the right hand side was written Albert Jules.'

I stayed very quiet for my own reasons.

'Must be a relative' Jean Paul said.

'That's what I thought but I saw the photos that the Pertwees were showing around and he was bloody well in one of those photos, or someone who looked like him -almost identical. Incredible eh?' Gerard laughed.

'Oohhh that's spooky, ' Linda shuddered and shivered, 'feels like someone just walked across my grave, as my dear old Mum used to say.'

'Now, did you know,' Jean Paul cut in 'that in France, when they say that, the phrase does not refer to your future grave but to a past grave.'

'A past grave?' Gerard repeated.

'Yes, a past grave. Someone who believes that they have already lived or their soul has inhabited other people's bodies previously. The shudder comes just after they are reminded of a dream that is a vision of their past.'

'Really? Gerard smiled

'Yes, really. Now in Ireland,' Jean Paul continued now in full flow, 'people used to say that they feel like a goose has just walked over my grave. This being some sort of premonition rather than a past life experience and it's where the term goosebumps comes from.'

Jean Paul looked at us all triumphantly and we all broke into a spontaneous applause at the man who never let us down with his stories and knowledge.

Chapter 12 – Beatrice and her friends

Our usual gang of three – Gerard, Jean Paul and myself were joined by Didier and of course Linda, once again at the bar.

We were going over everything that we had discovered from talking with Eric Gautier. About his life with and without his wife Beatrice.

We had learnt that Eric's wife Beatrice Gautier was pretty close for a time with a couple of women friends. Eric knew them but not very well. One of them lived in St Pierre but Eric hardly ever saw her and the other lived outside the village.

As it turned out Linda knew one of them, through a mutual friend. Linda had taken it upon herself to go and see her when she spotted her in the queue at the butchers shop. Her name was Caroline and the brief conversation was rather disjointed, as this woman, Caroline could not take her eyes off of handsome Claude, the butcher.

Linda recounted her conversation with Caroline, who had explained that she was always a little distant with Beatrice as she found her quite a difficult person. What she did remember was that Beatrice used to talk about another woman, whose name she could not now remember. This woman lived out in the countryside on an old farm that was really isolated. She was one of those women who was into esoteric stuff – you know healing through the powers of the mother earth, chanting at certain times of the year, empowerment through meditation and offerings. That kind of herbalist thing'

'What kind of thing?' Gerard asked.

'Making up potions, herbal stuff, capturing moon beams in a bottle and selling them'

'Moonbeams in a bottle!' exclaimed Didier.

'I know, that sounds a little wacky doesn't it?'

'Wacky to say the least', Didier said again.

'Not unlike holy water' Jean Paul smiled.

'What?' Didier turned to Jean Paul.

'Holy water – ordinary tap water, bottled and blessed by a priest'. Jean Paul suggested.

'Bloody hell, I had not thought of it like that'. Didier confessed.

'Well we all seem to be lapsed Catholics around these parts, maybe the holy water was not blessed enough?' Gerard laughed.

'But moonbeams in a bottle – come on?' Didier shrugged trying to get back to the conversation in point

Gerard and I broke into song spontaneously.

'Would you like to swing on a star
Carry moonbeams home in a jar
And be better off than you are

Or would you rather be a mule'

'Bing Crosby, swing on a star,' Jean Paul stated.

'Listen,' Didier interrupted our temporary mirth and said, 'Eric Gaultier told us that Beatrice was getting into this stuff more and more as they became more and more distant. Her friend Caroline here in the village was decidedly odd but the one out in the countryside was bonkers. I mean certifiably bonkers and not a little scary. He stayed away from her as much as he could. He was never invited out to see her. But on the rare occasions when she was around the village, he said he kept his distance and so did she, with him.'

Didier looked at Linda and started to speak again. 'You said that Caroline said that this woman made up potions – did she describe herself as a herbalist?'

'Oh yes most definitely,' Linda explained. She said that both her and Beatrice saw this woman as very knowledgeable about plants and treatments. She described herself as many things – herbalist, spiritualist, an earth goddess and plenty of other things, as I understood.'

'You did not like her?' Didier concluded.

'As I said, I never met her – she felt like a major influence on Caroline and Beatrice as time went on.'

They all sat there looking at one another until Jean Paul broke the silence.

'I know her name. It's Elspeth. Elspeth Brigande,' he explained.

'How do you know her?' Gerard asked.

'I had to go with a builder friend and fix her roof a few years ago. Rotten roof on an old farmhouse in the middle of nowhere.'

'You never said as we were all trying to think who she might be,' Gerard complained.

'Best left well alone in my opinion. Mad as a hatter but she does not call herself Elspeth. She goes by the name Alara,' Jean Paul explained further.

'Alara?'

'Alara – apparently it means all powerful in Celtic. My mate got a right tongue lashing off her for calling her Elspeth. I kept my head down and my mouth shut. She scared the shit out of me. Apparently, she has a website where she describes herself as an earth goddess and promotes female freedom and development and offers weekend sanctuaries for women who want self empowerment'. Jean Paul explained.

'How do you know this?' Didier asked.

'My mate's sister sort of became involved but drew the line at bottling moonbeams while being naked and chanting at the new moon, apparently,' Jean Paul simply explained.

'Apparently? You sound very well informed? ' Gerard smirked at Jean Paul, 'I'm surprised you didn't join them. Sounds right up your street'.

'It's interesting this Caroline could not remember her name,' Linda added.

'Or chose not to remember her name,' Gerard replied.

'I need to think how to handle this', Didier thought out aloud. There are connections here that need to be explored. Vincent Duval was poisoned. That was the coroner's conclusion. That poison was very likely a hemlock. Eric Gautier, living in the same village was also poisoned with hemlock that was thankfully for him, not fatal. Eric's wife Beatrice then simply disappears off the face of the earth. Now we have an earth goddess living not far from here, who amongst other things describes herself as a herbalist and apart from the dead man, Vincent Duval, they all knew this Elspeth or Alara.'

'Maybe Vincent Duval knew her as well but we can't ask him,' Gerard commented

We all kept silent, so as not to disturb the ex Inspector's train of thought.

Neither this Alara aka Elspeth nor Beatrice came up in the investigation of Mr Duval's murder, so I think I need to contact the Inspector, who took over from me when I retired'.

'Sounds like a plan Didier', Gerard agreed.

Chapter 13 – the dinner invitation

So a week after discovering the Stein, Janine and Arthur Barnes thought that an invitation to the American guy, Bill Brown would be a nice idea. Bill was more than happy to accept the invitation.

Over dinner, Janine and Arthur, not unlike the Pertwees, went through their usual line of questioning, some would say interrogation process – who, what, where and when. Gerard would always call them nosey bastards but he was not English and did not understand the English middle class and their seemingly endless ability to want to know everything there was about anyone.

Bill ate his way through a seafood salad, which was not easy as he was always uneasy with anything with a shell on it and then steered his way around the peas and cauliflower, as he was not an admirer of most vegetables apart from sweet corn and broccoli. Luckily there was beef and there was roast potatoes and gravy, so he ate that with great relish (well English mustard as it happened).

It was over the cheese course and a very nice port that Janine asked Bill about his collection of Steins that he had. Bill explained that he had had a fascination for collecting them, when he was living in America. Since he had been living in France, he had not found any. He explained that he had started off with four that he had inherited from his parents, which they bought with them back in 1037 when they emigrated to America.

Janine leapt up excitedly and ran to the kitchen and returned with the cleaned up Stein that she had found.

'I discovered it in an old hidden cupboard last week at the back of the house. It must have been left here from the war'. She handed them to Bill who looked at and recognised the markings on it from a town somewhere in Bavaria.

'Wow, that's super. It's a lovely design,' Bill said.

'Well, it is yours,' Janine said spontaneously.

Bill went to refuse but Janine was insistent and so after a thoroughly pleasant evening, apart from some of the food, he departed with the stein and an acknowledgement that he was a fussy bastard when it came to food.

His dietary pleasures of steak that fell apart with the slice of a knife and peanut butter and jelly sandwiches seemed a long way off in the States.

It was his next conversation with Janine and Arthur as to who might have left a Stein behind that was to open up another world to him.

Chapter 14 – More disturbing news

We called another meeting.

We were still reeling from what to do and say to the Professor over the photographs, which were odd to say the least. We had recovered the stolen Bugatti to its rightful owner, but now, we seemed to be looking at a serial hemlock poisoner and murderer. Didier, Gerard, Jean Paul and myself sat at the bar. We had chosen an afternoon when Linda was going into town to do her shopping, so that finally Jean Paul was on his own.

Didier and Gerard ran through everything they had discussed with Eric and what the evidence was for the murder of Vincent Duval.

'Did you know they reckoned Socrates' death was down to hemlock?' Jean Paul attested.

'Really' Gerard replied looking sceptical.

' Oh yes', Jean Paul continued 'Plato wrote about it in his book the Phaedo – he was forced to drink an infusion of hemlock. Medical experts say that his centripel paralysis was a characteristic of that poison'.

'Well I never cease to be amazed with your knowledge Jean Paul' quipped Gerard, 'Dare I ask why he was forced to drink this infusion?'

'Essentially, he was found guilty of telling young people that they should not believe in the Gods. He was guilty of sedition I guess?'

'That's your contribution to this investigation? Fucking Socrates,'

Gerard complained to Jean Paul.

'I thought you might like to know that. Someone had to find out about hemlock. Clearly it was a favoured method back with the Ancient Greeks. I doubt if the Greeks were alone in knowing and using it as a well known method of poisoning. Probably well before them and afterwards. The fact that someone is doing it today is no surprise – modern day witches, sorry herbalists did not just invent it'.

'Ideed not' Didier agreed.

'So now we have three problems to solve,' Gerard shrugged.

'Three?' Didier asked.

'Yes' Gerard started picking up his empty glass and then said 'four actually.'

'Four?' questioned Jean Paul

'Firstly we have a murder to help solve. Secondly, we have the disappearance of one Beatrice Gautier to solve. Three, what to do about the fact that the Professor appears to have been around this village for the last 150 years.' Gerard hesitated, 'Oh and then there is a fourth'.

'A fourth?' Jean Paul asked again.

'Yes a fourth,' he said and turned to Jean Paul with his empty glass, 'whose round is it Jean Paul?'

Very funny Gerard' Jean Paul nodded good heartedly and shouted for Marcel for a *'la meme chose*' – same again.

'So the murderer must have been local to have poisoned both Eric and this Duval character,' Jean Paul turned serious, 'which means that they are either walking around today, whether they are a local resident to St Pierre or elsewhere, who knows? Its kind of scary thinking we might know them or have met them.'

'It's what we tell our children – be careful of strangers but more often than not, it's the people you know and think you are safe with that do the harm.' Gerard reflected.

' That's right.,' Didier agreed, 'there are the random killers and the very occasional serial killer but they are rare and that's why the media make such a song and dance about it but normally it is a family member, friend or a neighbour.'

Chapter 15 – Detective Chief Inspector Isabelle Dupont

The next morning, Ex Inspector Didier Lauren telephoned his old colleague, now Detective Chief Inspector Isabelle Dupont. Isabelle Dupont had a reputation for diplomacy whilst not suffering fools gladly, whether they be criminals, suspects, witnesses or fellow officers. Coupled with this direct talking was a sense of humour second to none. This was all wrapped up in a sense of timing that made her a formidable detective, colleague and friend.

She was fire arm trained of course and enjoyed kick boxing as her relaxing sport or exercise of choice. Isabelle Dupont was best summed up as the 'Iron fist in the velvet glove.' She was determined and forceful, hidden under a gentle exterior. Isabelle always smiled at this as it was Emperor Napoleon Bonaparte who is often credited with having used the expression to signify that firmness can be couched with outwards gentleness and it was good enough for her if it was good enough for Napoleon.

Isabelle's colleague and assistant, Quincy Rochefort could not have been more different. Not as tall as Isabelle and not as quick to be roused, he was a perfect foil to his boss. He also hated the name Quincy, more so after most people who met him asked if his parents named him after the American TV series Quincy, which was a medical detective series. Quincy preferred the idea of people seeing him more as a more laid back Quincy Jones the musician. Unfortunately Quincy was about the same height as the actor Jack Klugman, who played Quincy the TV coroner. Quincy Rochefort was also not black. He was not only white but a very pale white, as he disliked being in the sun, so he was never convincing trying to associate with a cool talented black musician.

Isabelle had suggested that Didier come over and meet with them. This he did straight away. When Didier arrived at Isabelle's office, she explained that they were just waiting for Quincy to join them.

'He may be a few minutes I'm afraid. He has been somewhat delayed.' Isabelle explained.

'Nothing serious, I hope,' Didier asked.

'Oh no nothing unusual. As you will remember my dear Didier, Quincy has certain, how shall I say? Routines. Routines to go through each and every day. Routines to perform?' Isabelle explained, waving her hands and arms around in a half explanatory and half apologetic way and raising her eyebrows.

'Oh yes, ' Didier suddenly acknowledged, remembering 'the toilet?'

'Yes, the toilet. He is on the toilet. As you will recall, it is a bodily function he seems unable to perform with any speed, I'm afraid.' Isabelle explained, 'and one that seems scheduled at exactly between 09.00 and 09.15 hours.

'Not to worry,' Didier smiled.'

'Oh but I do – with Quincy I have had to learn that patience is a virtue. You must remember Quincy, he cannot leave home without having his bowl of cornflakes and then when he arrives for work he must complete his major morning ablutions. Once he has completed his toiletry tasks then he magically transforms into a very able and sharp detective.

But I should not speak bad of an absent colleague.'

Didier smiled at the memory of Quincy. He did in fact remember that with a full bowel he was useless at solving crime or even being able to think coherently.

'I blame it on his upbringing as a child,' Isabelle shrugged. 'However, mission accomplished then he is up there with the best.'

'On company time too Chief Inspector? You are very accommodating,' Didier smiled.

'As you were, if I recall, ex Inspector Lauren,' Isabelle reminded him.

Any further conversation was cut short as Detective Quincy Rochefort entered the room. Isabelle pointed to the table and chairs in her office and the three of them sat down.

Quincy Rochefort did look to Didier, like a man who was neither unburdened and fully concentrated.

'I have invited Didier to this meeting to discuss the unsolved murder of Vincent Duval. Didier, as you know, was in charge of the investigation until I took over. He has information that may be relevant to the case'.

Didier talked through the chance discovery of the missing Bugatti and the subsequent conversation with Eric Gaultier and the fact that he too was poisoned, but not fatally, just before Vincent Duval was killed. Both were poisoned with water hemlock.

They agreed that the hemlock was either naturally growing somewhere in St Pierre, that they had both visited, or they had both been poisoned on purpose.

The wife of Eric Gaultier, whose name was Beatrice Gaultier, was still living with him when he was poisoned. They were still together when Vincent Duval was murdered. Then Beatrice Gaultier just left and seemingly disappeared. Eric Gaultier has had no contact with her since nor can discover where she went. He never reported her missing as he considered that she had left him. To this day, her disappearance has never been reported to the Gendarmes by her husband Eric, nor anyone else.

This disappearance now needed to be treated as suspicious.

Didier then went on to talk about a friend of Beatrice whose name was Elspeth Brigande, who went by the name of Alara, which meant in Celtic 'all powerful.' She apparently considers herself a white witch.

'I am afraid I cannot enlighten you more about this woman, as I am not conversant with the practices of such a person, nor understand fully what a white witch is and what a white witch can do. All I know is that she supposedly makes potions and casts spells and that sort of stuff.' Didier explained.

Both the Chief Inspector and the Detective Inspector then reviewed the case file with Didier, which revealed virtually nothing of any use. It was as if all evidence other than the poison had been sucked into a black hole. No witnesses, no motives, nothing.

'This is the first possible new line of inquiry. We will need to formally interview Eric Gaultier about his poisoning and the disappearance of his wife Beatrice. We will also need to interview this Elspeth to see if she has anything to do with the hemlock poisoning or knows what happened to Beatrice,' Isabelle concluded.

Quincy left them to go and find the address of Elspeth Brigande.

'Thank you Didier,' Isabelle smiled at Didier, 'it does not seem much of a lead but at least it is something fresh and new after all these years. I will keep you informed of anything we uncover.'

She shook Didier's hand and with that he left the gendarmerie pleased with the fact that the lead was being followed up.

Didier drove back to La Croix de Bois, where he invited Gerard, Jean Paul and myself to meet with him. Linda of course was with Jean Paul. Over a round of coffees, it was agreed that Didier and Gerard should go and talk with Cristal Lamar, the beautiful Pharmacist, which of course was always a pleasure. As a pharmacist, she was also a qualified Doctor. We considered her also as a general mystic and healer. We were all in agreement that Cristal was the one person that we all knew, who seemed to know about these sorts of things, would be able to recognise hemlock and understand its uses.

We agreed to meet up in two days' time, where they had organised a botanist walk around the village of St Pierre to look for hemlock. This included Didier, Gerard, Jean Paul and Linda, Cristal and myself.

Two days later, we gathered in the small car park near the church. Cristal called us round in a group.

'Now' she started, 'what we are looking for is hemlock. The stems have reddish or purple spots and streaks. The leaves are bright green and fern like, they look serrated and are finely divided. The flowers are tiny and a lovely white, arranged in a small, umbrella shaped cluster on the ends of the stems. They have a strong musty odour to them when they are crushed' and she then handed out a photo of the plant to each of us.

'What happens if we touch a hemlock by mistake?' Linda asked Cristal

'Well try not to. Some people may get a rash if they have sensitive skin but hemlock is usually only poisonous if it is ingested.'

'So it is unlikely that Vincent Duvall or poor Eric were poisoned just by touching it?' Didier asked.

'It's possible but highly unlikely' Cristal answered.

'And what does it smell like without crushing it as you said?' Linda asked.

'Well, interestingly, it smells like very sweet parsley. It is known as spotted parsley or spotted cowbane and is from the carrot family'.

'And it is known as the suicide root by the Iroquois Indians' Jean Paul chipped in.

Gerard and I laughed at Jean Paul's latest bit of information.

So we set off in pairs walking around the village to the fields at the edge of the village. It was a pleasant sunny late afternoon and after a couple of hours, we all met back at the car park. None of us had found any evidence of hemlock.

'Well that solves that avenue of investigation then' Gerard summed up.

' I'm for searching the witch's place' Jean Paul proposed.

" We can't just go and walk into her house and garden', Didier said, waving his arms in mock protest.

'Yes of course we can' Jean Paul argued, ' we simply wait until she is not there and we go in and do a search'.

'That's not right nor legal', Didier argued.

'We did it at Guys Cliffe before we broke in there,' Jean Paul stated, reminding us of a previous adventure that nearly turned out badly.

'And yes, look what happened, we got caught' Gerard answered

'Well we won't get caught this time. You' Jean Paul said pointing at Gerard, ' Cristal and myself will go in wherever it is she lives and Linda and you,' pointing at me can be lookouts either side of where she lives. Didier, you should not be involved'.

We all looked at each other and there was no dissent.

'That's a plan then' Jean Paul concluded.

On the way back to La Croix de Bois, it was getting dark. Jean Paul stopped us and looked up at the evening sky. The brightest stars were beginning to twinkle.

'Look' Jean Paul declared, 'behold the stars. The milky way may well be visible tonight.'

"Looks like a wispy cloud to me,' Gerard replied.

Jean Paul gave him a withering look that was lost in the gathering gloom.

'And Voyager 2 is out there.'

'Where?' Gerard asked.

'You can't see it stupid. It was launched in 1984 or thereabouts and it is now only just leaving our solar system. Incredible eh? It takes 18 hours for a message to get from Voyager to earth and 18 hours to send an answer back.' Jean Paul was waxing, ' but its not met a single other entity, nor message nor evidence of anything out there. Hubble is the same. Lots of wonderful photographs but not a single form of life. I find that troubling.'

'Troubling in what way?' Gerard asked.

'Troubling that it appears that there is no one out there. That we are all alone in this universe.'

'Well it is a big place. Someone might show up.' Gerard suggested trying to sound optimistic.

'Perhaps we have to understand the astrophysicists.'

Gerard turned to me and although I could not clearly see his face in the dark, I knew what kind of face he was pulling and the eyebrows were being raised, for we both knew what was coming.

'Some astrophysicists have postulated that there are more than likely an infinite number of parallel universes that exist alongside ours and all had the same starting point but have evolved differently. Some have ceased to exist and some have developed in totally different ways.'

'So somewhere parallel to us are the five of us currently discussing the same improbable questions in another space and time?'

'Exactly,' Jean Paul agreed and then stopped. 'Well probably variations of us, as there are infinite options.'

'What a scary thought,' Gerard said. 'Infinite options for you Jean Paul. That is probably the scariest thing that I have ever had to contemplate.'

I thought the same but chose to remain quiet. Trying to understand my life in La Croix de Bois and its many dynamics and happenings was more than my head could cope with, never mind the infinite variations of Jean Paul.

Chapter 16 – the search

We all agreed that it would be helpful for Inspector Isabelle Dupont to do this before she went to visit Elspeth aka Alara Brigande to interview her. We all made inquiries as innocently as we could with people we knew to try and find the address of this woman. Being rural and local, we had no trouble in locating where she lived. This avoided Didier having to have any conversation with Chief Inspector Isabelle Dupont, who we also agreed was best left in the dark in relation to our proposed plan.

We all agreed that it was for the best to not only keep this plan from the Chief Inspector but also everyone else. This was going to be strictly between ourselves. We had managed this quite successfully in the past. I guess we had become a tight little gang, a cohort of mystery solvers.

Jean Paul delegated himself to carry out the reconnaissance on the house and asked Gerard to drive him out there.

Like a well oiled military machine, Jean Paul and Gerard found some good positions where we could hide or wait without raising any concerns, where we could leave cars or bikes to alert one another. What we realised is that we would have to take pot luck as to her movements, as none of us knew any of her schedules nor possible visitors.

'I would not even like to imagine what kinds of people might be visiting this woman' Jean Paul said with a shudder.

It was also agreed that such a search would have to take place in the evening as Cristal was working in the pharmacy all that week. We also proposed that Didier as an ex Inspector should not come with us. He did not need to sully a near perfect career in law enforcement, being caught with a group of reprobates sneaking illegally around someone's house and garden.

The first evening that we chose, we had to keep on the move to avoid being observed as two women showed up at the house and left after about twenty minutes. We were all a bit wary, so agreed to try the next evening.

As luck would have it that next evening, a Tuesday around seven o'clock Elspeth, aka Alara the powerful, climbed into her car and drove off.

"We have a go at nineteen hundred hours. I say again we are clear to enter' Jean Paul whispered into his mobile phone to Linda.

'Copy that,' Gerard replied and then added, 'we are good to go,' in his best American accent he could do. 'Bravo team is on the move,' he laughed, in the hope of winding Jean Paul up.

We immediately jumped into action. Linda drove up the road to where Elspeth (Alara) had driven off and parked by the first set of crossroads, from where she could telephone a warning with as much notice as possible.

I drove down to the house and dropped Cristal, Jean Paul and Gerard off by the entrance to her house and then drove back to where we had been observing her.

The house was an old farm house – two old cottages that had been converted into one. There was a small barn and two outbuildings and a garden. The nearest neighbour was about 300 metres down a small road. It was isolated.

Cristal had explained that they were looking in the garden and the outbuildings only, so there was no need for Jean Paul to come armed with any tools for breaking in anywhere else.

Cristal said she would take the garden and Jean Paul and Gerard the outbuildings. Gerard and Jean Paul pushed the door to the first outbuilding which looked like it used to house pigs and it was half filled with stacked wood. They then crossed over to the barn which contained a variety of tools, axes and garden pots and bags. There were bales of hay and some old discarded wooden furniture that looked centuries old.

They walked over to the last outbuilding and opened the door. It was darker and more dingy than the first building. Jean Paul froze in front of Gerard.

Gerard looked over Jean Paul's shoulder.

'What the fuck?' he exclaimed immediately. There in front of them, on a long old dining table were two knives – one white handled and one black. Besides them was a whip and two pots. On the ground were a number of cauldrons of different sizes. Hanging up from the beams were bundles of herbs and plants tied off and upside down.

Just past the table on the dirt floor was the markings of a shape drawn in the earth.

'Is that what I think it is?' Gerard asked.

'It looks like a pentangle to me' Jean Paul answered, 'And these he continued, pointing at the objects on the table, 'I have never seen such things before but I looked some stuff up on the internet yesterday so I knew just in case, what I might be looking for as evidence.. The white handled knife is called a Boline. It's a special knife used in rituals but don't ask me what rituals. The article just said rituals,' he explained

'And the black one?' Gerard asked.

'I think it's called an Athame, which is described as a ceremonial knife. The difference between a ceremonial knife and a ritual knife, I do not have a clue but it can't be good.'

'And the whip? Gerard asked, pointing at the very item.

'Oh my God,' Jean Paul exclaimed, 'this whip is called a scourge, which according to the same article I read on the internet is used as a punishment in certain rituals'.

'Oh fucking hell,' was all Gerard could manage.

'Indeed' Jean Paul agreed with his good friend, 'whose idea was it to come out here?'

'The pots and containers on the ground look like the sort of things for burning incense in, like in the church.' Gerard observed

'Hey guys', came the sudden voice behind them and Jean Paul

and Gerard grabbed one another, startled.

It was Cristal.

'What's up with you two hugging one another - are you having a secret tryst in here?' She asked and then saw what they had been looking at.

'OK', she said, picking up the Boline and looking at the Athame and the Scourge, 'pretty standard stuff for a witch, I would say. Let's go'

'What about looking for hemlock? Jean Paul asked.

'Found some. It's there over towards the boundary by the trees and the field, along a very small stream. There is actually quite a lot of it.'

Gerard and Jean Paul needed no encouragement. Gerard phoned me to get me to come down and pick them up. At the same time, Jean Paul's telephone rang. Jean Paul turned to Cristal and Gerard, 'she's on her way back – she is just about to drive past Linda.'

The three of them ran down the drive to the road and turned left and started up the first part of it. It ran straight for some 150 to 200 metres, so they had no way of not being seen if she came towards them. They heard a car coming down the hill winding its way towards the house.

'What should we do?' Cristal asked.

'Get in the car' Jean Paul said as calmly as you could imagine. Jean Paul might have been cursed with many odd traits but there was nothing wrong with his eyesight. He had seen me driving towards them. I screeched to a halt, as I too had seen this Alara returning, from where I had stopped previously.

They opened the doors and climbed in. It was too late to turn around, so I calmly drove towards the oncoming car and pulled over as she passed waving as I did. Alara, the self proclaimed white witch, neither waved nor looked at us and we drove away to meet up with Linda. Jean Paul and Linda had been apart for nearly 25 minutes, so they would need reuniting.

The next day, armed with the knowledge from an 'anonymous tip off' that there was hemlock growing in Elspeth Brigandes back garden, Chief Inspector Isabelle Dupont, Inspector Quincy Rochefort and two gendarmes headed for Alara, the powerful's, residence.

Chapter 17 - The Interview

Isabelle and Quincy knocked on the door and they were answered by a woman in her fifties with long greyish hair that was tied back. She had what can only be described as a pale complexion. In time, Jean Paul would come to describe her as someone who looked like she had had a bath in white paint and she reminded him of Casper the ghost.

She also had piercing green eyes.

'Yes' she answered.

'Elspeth Brigande?' Isabelle asked.

'No' came the reply.

'Oh sorry, Alara Brigande?' Isabelle asked again.

'Who wants to know and who are you?' She snapped.

'This is Inspector Quincy Rochefort and I am Chief Inspector Isabelle Dupont. We are here in connection with the murder of Vincent Duval and something that may or may not be connected, the disappearance of Beatrice Gaultier, both from the village nearby of St Pierre.'

'Never heard of either of them,' Alara replied.

'It was some time ago, so you may need to cast your memory back' Isabelle smiled politely.

'Nope, never heard of them.'

'Come now' Isabelle said. 'We know you and Beatrice were friends.'

'We were never friends,' Elspeth Brigande sneered.

'So you did know her or you've never heard of her?' Isabelle stared at her into her very green eyes. After a silent ten seconds, Elspeth replied.

'So I knew her. What about it?'

'Well friends or acquaintances I care not,' Isabelle stated, 'but you certainly knew and saw Beatrice before she disappeared. Perhaps, I should use the word – vanished. Because she certainly did and has not been seen since.'

'So?' Elspeth replied rather defiantly.

'So,' Isabelle continued, 'firstly, you do know her or know of her. Thank you for making that so easy,' Isabelle said sarcastically. 'Now having finally established that fact, secondly, you are living only some two kilometres from St Pierre. Now, it would be highly unusual that you would not have heard of the only murder in St Pierre, in both this century and the last for that matter. Vincent Duval is the name in everyone's heads as the man who was murdered in St Pierre.'

'Oh him' Elspeth replied.

'Yes him, Vincent Duvall. But thirdly, we know that Beatrice Gaultier and yourself were, how shall I put it? Known to one another. Shared certain esoteric interests?' Isabelle continued smiling and explaining her line of enquiry.

'Well, I can't help you. Sorry' and she went to close the door.

'OK, you have a choice Elspeth' Isabelle smiled, emphasising the word Elspeth. 'You can talk to us here, or we can arrange for a formal interview at the station, which will be recorded and may be used as evidence in our inquiries.'

Elspeth stood there looking at them.

'So', Isabelle smiled again, 'would you like to invite us in?'

Elspeth Brigande reluctantly beckoned them in.

They all sat down at the kitchen table. Isabelle explained that she was entitled to have legal representation if she thought it necessary. Elspeth declined the offer. Isabelle started to ask about Vincent Duval. Has she ever met him? Did she know of him? Elspeth denied ever knowing him. She then asked about her friendship with Beatrice and again, Elspeth was vague, she claimed she hardly knew her.

It was then that the Chief Inspector stated that other parties interviewed explained that Beatrice and another friend, Caroline spent a considerable amount of time with Elspeth and that they were part of a group who liked to practice a range of alternative therapies and treatments.

With her practices described like this Elspeth visibly relaxed a little and they discussed some of the group sessions and the empowerment for women procedures. The Chief Inspector agreed that she had sympathy with many women who struggled in a male dominated society or in difficult relationships.

'So do you know why Beatrice left her husband and then disappeared?' Isabelle asked.

'I knew she was unhappy but beyond that I did not know anything,' Elspeth answered.

'Were you not worried when she disappeared and no one could find her? If they had been unhappy, as you said they were, or should I say, Beatrice was, did you wonder if anything bad had happened to her?' Isabelle asked.

'No I did not. I was just pleased for her that she had left him'.

'He had been quite unwell in the months before she left him', Isabelle explained. As she said this, she looked intently into the green eyes of Elspeth aka, Alara the powerful and saw a slight twitch.

'I did not know that' Elspeth stated.

'Indeed, he had a series of illnesses that ended with him being taken into hospital. It was when he was in hospital that after tests, they confirmed that it was possible poisoning. Poisoning with hemlock'.

The Chief Inspector let the silence hang in the air and stared deeply into Elspeth's eyes again. The silence in the room was loud, which Isabelle broke after nothing was said for a full minute.

By a remarkable coincidence, Vincent Duval died a few months later of hemlock poisoning. Two men in the same village were both poisoned with hemlock. Incredible eh?'

'So?' She replied.

'So I wonder what you think about that?'

'So, it's terrible. What do you want me to say?' Elspeth countered.

'If I looked in your garden, would I find any hemlock plants?' Isabelle asked. 'I have been told that you do have hemlock in your garden Elspeth. Yet another coincidence'

Elspeth wriggled a little in her chair.

'What are you suggesting? That I'm some sort of poisoner?'

'I am simply saying that we have two men, one dead and one thankfully alive who were poisoned with hemlock. We can find no trace of the plant in the village nor surrounding fields and here we are on your premises and apparently, there are healthy hemlock plants in your garden. To add to that coincidence we also have a missing person, who was your friend or associate or whatever she was to you, she was certainly a member of your group. Or should we perhaps call it a coven?'

'Coven? What are you accusing me of now?' Elspeth shouted.

'We can call it whatever you want to call it. I'm going to go with coven for the time being. If I was to search your premises, as part of our ongoing murder and missing person investigation, I would also very likely find the tools and evidence of how you practice your beliefs and your ceremonies and rituals as part of your coven', Isabelle stated taking a gamble.

'You've been snooping around my premises when you have no right to'.

'Let me assure you, I have not nor have any of my officers been on these premises before. However we do know that there are such things on your premises told to us by third parties. Frankly I don't care what you practice in the privacy of your own home but a friend of yours is missing. She could even be dead for all we know. Maybe,' Isabelle paused, trying to create a dramatic effect. 'Maybe, she was also poisoned. Maybe she is also dead from hemlock poisoning?'

'How dare you' Elspeth spat

'Just like those two men'. Isabelle concluded, 'but as you have stated, you only knew one vaguely as the husband of one of your friends or member of your group or coven. Sorry to use that term again but I cannot think of a different term for the time being.'

They sat there looking at one another. Elspeth's face was venomous.

'And the other gentleman, you say you never knew and had never heard of, despite being a local man who had been murdered and was the talk of the area, never mind the village of St Pierre.'

Both Isabelle and Quincy could hear Elspeth muttering under her breath. A curse no doubt thought Isabelle but she maintained her steely stare at the white witch.

'Now Madam Brigande, shall we ask if my colleague Inspector Roquefort can have a look around your premises or do I need to get a search warrant?' Isabelle smiled.

'Go and get a search warrant.'

'OK. In that case I must inform you that I am arresting you in connection with the possible poisoning of two men, one of which was fatal and in connection with the disappearance of Beatrice Gautier'.

'It wasn't me. I curse you.'

Isabelle just managed to stop herself saying out aloud that she thought that she had already been cursed by her. She smiled instead.

Quincy Roquefort handcuffed the woman and nodded his head when Isabelle asked him to request a search warrant to have an officer sent to the house to guard it until the search warrant and officers were organised.

They both marched her to the car, listening to various incantations and curses. These continued all the way to the Gendarmerie and into the cell.

'When her curses were finally silenced by the door to her cell being slammed shut, Quincy turned to Isabelle and said

'Nice one Chief'.

Isabelle nodded. Whether Elspeth Brigande was guilty of murder and poisoning and the disappearance of Beatice Gaultier, she did not know. However, Elspeth aka Alara Brigande still knew an awful lot more and had much to tell them.

In the afternoon, there was a knock on Isabelle's door. It was Quincy.

'Chief, some news. Beatrice Gaultier is not dead, or should I say wasn't dead seven years ago. Her carte vitale (*the French national health card that everyone has*) was used down in Toulouse, according to their records.'

'OK' Isabelle replied, 'do we know what she was being treated for?'

'It certainly was not a hospital admission or doctor,' Quincy answered.

'Not poisoning then?'

'No it wasn't. Strangely enough, she was having some kind of hormone treatment, it would seem,' Quincy stated.

'What for?'

'I'm not sure but I'm trying to find out. In our process of searching for any records on Beatrice Gaultier, it was a bit slow as we had to flag it through the health payment system, because nothing is showing up on any tax or health records for the last seven years. When we asked about this treatment they explained that they are going to have to look at the files to see where the treatment was, what it was for and by whom.'

'Excellent.' Isabelle replied.

'It's strange that there is just no record of her since this treatment seven years ago and there was nothing before this treatment and when she left her husband. Nothing, no employment records, no tax, no addresses, no accidents, incidents. Nothing.' Quincy continued.

'As if she disappeared as Beatrice Gaultier completely and on purpose,' Isabelle suggested.

'Exactly,' Quincy agreed.

'Thank you. Keep me posted.' Isabelle asked.

Chapter 18 – the ongoing aftermath of the 'breeze'

I joined Gerard, Jean Paul and Linda for an evening glass of wine. They were sitting looking at the butcher shop. The door was open and there was a queue that was from the counter to outside the door. They were all women, apart from one man and all of them were looking inwards including the man.

'Handsome Claude is doing a roaring trade this evening' Jean Paul commented.

'He does every evening,' I said.

'That's because everyone is in love with him' Linda said.

'He's also a pretty good butcher as well,' Gerard pointed out.

'He was always popular but now he is inundated' Jean Paul added

'He's the most handsome man in this town', said Linda, 'no offence Jean Paul or to you both either'.

'He's always been handsome like Claude but the attraction to him seems to have gone nuclear recently.' Gerard added and he turned to Linda and Jean Paul 'it seems to have happened around the same time you too were suddenly smitten with one another', Gerard added.

I went in to order a second round of drinks and spoke to Marcel the bar owner who was washing glasses in the sink.

'What's happened to the dishwasher? Do you not use it any more?' I asked.

'Not since it exploded on me that day. No I bloody well don't,' came the reply, 'I'll bring the drinks out to you'.

I went back to sit with my friends and pondered the events following the 'breeze' including the stolen Bugatti and the ongoing investigation into the poisoning of both Eric and Vincent Gautier. There definitely seemed like some sort of connection but it was hard to make any sense of it. Well, the logical part of me said that it made no sense. What was that breeze I heard myself thinking. The Professor had whispered about it being 'the special wind' but I had paid little heed to that at the time.

Another thing that was happening that I was only to become aware of at a later date was to Bill Brown the American following the discovery of the Stein that Janine Barnes had found in her house, the so-called Gestapo house.

Chapter 19 - A most welcome Reunion

Bill Brown's parents had left Germany in 1937 to America. Bill's father, Gerd, was German and his mother, Rosa was Jewish. The anti semitism in Germany was rife and the writing was on the wall, often literally, in the new fatherland. They had both been born in Dresden but had moved west across Germany to Cologne for work. They had settled in well and as an engineer Gerd, had thrived, ironically building armoured tanks. However, life was increasingly uncomfortable for them.

When they had arrived in America, work was easy to find and he soon managed to secure an almost identical job, but in the car industry. Rosa had also found work as an administrator in the same factory. Gerd called himself Gerald but never Gerry because the derivation into Gerry even without the J for Jerry did not seem a sensible option.

As a German, he was not signed into the Army to fight in the Second World War. By 1940, Gerald and Rosa were residents of the United States among more than 1.2 million people who had been born in Germany. There were 5 million more who had two native-German parents, and 6 million who had one native-German parent.

Gerald was not deemed to be a risk and therefore was not detained although some 11,000 mostly German nationals were, alongside many Japanese.

They had raised two kids, a daughter they named Rosanna who was the eldest and a son, whom they named after his brother,

Wilhelm. He was christened as Wilhelm on the birth certificate but everyone called him Willie, rather than the German spelling Wilhelm. Wilhelm preferred the name Bill rather than Willie. Once he left home at eighteen he introduced himself to everyone as Bill. Naturally, his parents still liked to call him Wilhelm.

When Wilhelm's father Gerd left Germany, Gerd and his brother Wilhelm were destined to never meet again. As the war reached its conclusion Wilhelm Brun had simply surrendered along with the rest of the German garrison at Lorient. It took many months for him to return to Germany along with his remaining 'boys'. He returned home to Dresden, which had virtually been bombed flat. Wilhelm, living in Dresden, on the east side of Germany, which was under Russian occupation, found himself now living in a new country called East Germany behind the Berlin Wall.

He was destined to live a very different life to those of his fellow countrymen in West Germany and of course his brother Gerd living in America.

Wilhelm lived to see the Berlin Wall come down on the 9th November 1989. He was 79 years of age and poured a beer into his favourite stein and wondered what had happened to the matching stein that he had taken with him to France all those years back and had left it there.

He died in the following February having just reached 80 years. He had married in 1948 but his wife had passed away two years before him and he left three children, two daughters, Ursula and Ingrid and a son, Gunther.

When the wall fell they had all gathered together to join their father in toasting the wall coming down.

Of course Bill Brown and Janine Barnes were oblivious to such a tale. Janine had had a coffee with Bill the week afterwards and Bill had thanked her again for the Stein. Janine had told him about the history of the house and guessed that one of the soldiers must have left it there.

'I must tell you that last week I went to the Mayor's office to ask more about these houses. As you know and as everyone knows I've always hated the connection people make with this house and the Gestapo but one of the Mayor's assistants was terribly helpful and showed me some documents about this place.' Janine explained and took a breath.

'Please stop me if you want me to but I did discover that the commanding officer stationed here had the surname Brun. Commander Brun. He was not Gestapo, just regular army,' she hurriedly explained, 'and I thought that was a nice coincidence with you having a surname Brown.'

That made Bill sit up.

'And you being Mr Brown,' she continued nervously, 'which would be a derivation of Brun, I think?' She smiled.

So long story short, Bill and Janine go and see the secretary at the Mayor's office and make an appointment to come back later in the week when she has had time to find all the paperwork connected to the house.

The paperwork was illuminating. Wilhelm Brun was the

commander and had hailed from Dresden. Over the next few weeks Bill spent time on the internet searching for the name 'Brun' from Dresden. Of course, it was hard to track down anything from East Germany up until the mid 80's although he was informed by one very helpful researcher from the University of Dresden that the paperwork was very precise but had never been transposed onto the computer.

The researcher promised to get back to them but that Bill had to understand that there were an awful lot of Brun's to look through and the paperwork was mostly non existant.

The researcher did reply to him after around a week. Diligently he had slowly gone through Wilhelm Brun who fitted the time span and eventually discovered that a possible candidate who had survived the war had passed away in 1990. He had been in the army. Wilhelm Brun had three children, Ursula, Ingrid and Gunther.

He had no addresses for the children but suggested that Bill looked on Facebook and through the internet to look for the children, who would all now be just a little younger than Bill. He decided to try Gunther as he was the most likely to have kept the surname Brun as his sisters may well have married and taken new surnames.

After a few failed attempts he was able to track down a Gunther Brun, who seemed to fit the profile.

With great nervousness, Bill wrote to Gunther, making a friend request and explained who he was and that their Father had a brother called Gerd who had fled to America with Rosa in 1937, who were his parents. He must have written the draft ten different times because he thought it all sounded rather strange. Finally satisfied, he pressed send.

The next morning, there was nothing and neither did the evening bring any response. In fact the next three days, he heard nothing and began to see it as a dead end. Then on Saturday morning, Bill opened his Facebook page to find a message from Gunther.

'Yes, Gerd was my uncle but I never met him. My Father was Wilhelm and he was a commander in the German army.' That was what the message said in perfect English and underneath was a telephone number and a second message. 'Please ring me on this number one evening at your convenience.'

From there the rest is history. Bill rang and spoke with a cousin that he had never met and afterwards, he received messages from Ursula and Ingrid, who had married and had new surnames which was why he only searched for Gunther originally.

One month later, Bill was on a flight to Germany and had an emotional meeting with his three cousins and their families and with the stein that had been left all those years ago and stood it next to the remaining Stein that his Uncle had left in Dresden.

The chances of Bill Brown settling in La Croix de Bois from America when he retired in the exact same village where his fathers brother had kept the peace in a troubled time was incredible. The fact that a beer stein had reunited the two families over 75 years later was even better.

That wisp of air, that breeze or whatever it was had given up a happy secret with a happy conclusion. Something positive seventy five years later, coming from a dreadful time of war.

Chapter 20 – the confession of Elspeth Brigande

The search warrant had duly arrived and there had been a forensic search of the house owned by Elspeth Brigande.

Detective Quincy Rochefort was given the task of leading the search. Ironically, he had asked whether Cristal Lamar, the pharmacist, would be prepared to join him in the search for her expert advice.

Cristal was given the task of firstly looking to see if there was any hemlock growing in the garden. Quincy was struck at how quickly and proficiently, Cristal Lamar found the hemlock.

Indoors revealed further evidence of prepared mixtures of what looked like potions and tinctures arranged across a series of shelves. There was a whole wall of books, magazines and pamphlets and what looked like manuals with instructions. To Quincy, many of the books looked just like cookery books except the ingredients were not what the ordinary chef would put in a stew or in a curry.

What chilled him slightly was the discovery of a number of small dolls made with clay but with hair blended in. They were all lying in a set of draws. When they showed them to Cristal, she nodded and explained to the team that they were called 'poppets', which are dolls made to represent a specific person for the casting of spells on someone. The hair was likely real human hair. This hair, Cristal had explained, would have come from the person who was being cast a spell on, for it to work.

"Poppets or model dolls can be made from various materials', " she explained, "cloth stuffed with herbs, potatoes, corn cobs, carved roots. The idea is that any action that is performed on the poppet or effigy if you like, can be transferred to the person in question'.

'Like black magic?' an Officer asked.

'Not necessarily black magic. There are many who engage in such practices in the belief that it is more curative and helpful. To lift an illness or affliction from someone,' Cristal explained.

'So it is evidence of someone who practices magic that could be for good or bad?' Quincy asked.

'I guess, but maybe she just liked collecting them like toy dolls. Who can say until you ask her. I would imagine that along with everything else here, she would be practising these rituals both by herself and very probably with others'.

Cristal had read much about these practices as an accompanying interest to her medical training and as a pharmacist. It was intriguing for her as she had never seen such objects up close and of course the instructions for the tinctures and medicines were fascinating.

Upstairs they found an array of clothes, capes and masks. The Gendarmes showed a mix of excitement and more than a little uneasy because it all fitted in with their notions of what such witches and their followers wore.

Again, Cristal was keen to explain that they use the word practitioner and to explain that there has always been a theatrical side to such practices rather than see it as just an example of a coven.

She asked each of them what they thought of robed priests and some of the rituals that are practised every day in the Catholic church. This helped the two Gendarmes understand what they were looking at.

'Herbalists have been with us for millennia. They are the forefathers and mothers of people like me – pharmacists and before that we were known as apothacrists – people who simply prepares and sells drugs and compounds for medicinal purposes. Apothecary is a very old term that describes the production of healing remedies from raw materials such as herbs and plants. Indeed, believe it or not, it's true meaning is to describe a place where wine, spice and herbs were stored,' explained Cristal.

Quincy Rochefort was entranced listening to Cristal. He had become doe eyed looking at her. He was falling in love with the beautiful Cristal. She possessed a very fine mind and was rather attractive too.

An hour later, the gendarmes had finished their search and bagged up some of the containers with mixtures in them to take away for analysis.

Detective Rochefort drove Cristal Lamar back to the pharmacy at La Croix de Bois, besotted and in love and hopelessly tongue tied. In a daze, he then headed to the Gendarmerie to report to the Chief Inspector, ahead of an interview with Elspeth Brigande, aka Alara the powerful. Quincy went through what had been found at her house with his boss.

They entered the interview room and sat down with Elsepth Brigande.

The Chief Inspector formally introduced herself and Inspector Rochefort to Elspeth Brigande, the time and date and explained why she had been held in the cell.

'Let me be very clear,' Chief Inspector Isabelle Dupont started, 'We have searched your house and garden with a warrant and have taken away a number of your potions for testing. We have determined from the search that you are a practising herbalist and engage in a range of, how should I put it, magical and esoteric practices.'

Elspeth sat silently and glared at the Chief Inspector, who continued.

'I am not here to judge you on these practices. You are being held in custody because of the links now firmly evidenced, that you grow hemlock in your garden. Should the tests come back that hemlock is also found in any of the containers, then the current circumstantial evidence turns into strong evidence that links you to the poisoning of two men – one of whom died from hemlock poisoning. This puts you firmly within a charge of murder and attempted murder, to which you are looking at a life sentence,' Isabelle said slowly and softly.

'I did not know that the hemlock was growing...' Elspeth started to say but Isabelle cut her off.

'Please show some respect here and not waste all of our time with excuses like I did not know it was growing in my garden. I cannot stress to you enough that you need to cooperate in this investigation if you are to stand any chance of escaping a charge of accessory to murder, or even murder itself. You need to face up to the situation that you are in and either confess or help us to solve this murder.'

Isabelle stood up and Quincy followed suit, both standing behind the interview table.

'I shall be back in 10 minutes, while you consider your situation,' Isabelle explained and with that they both walked to the door and out of the room, closing the door behind them.

In the corridor, Isabelle turned to Quincy

'Do you have anything back from the doctors who treated Beatrice Gautier yet?'

'No, but I am chasing them up again this afternoon' Quincy replied.

'Good'.

They went and had a coffee and then returned to the interview room and sat down in front of Elspeth Brigande.

'So?' Isabelle said, 'what do you want to tell us?'

Elspeth Brigande fidgeted on her chair and then sat up straight.

'I want you to understand a few things. I am a herbalist and a healer. I define myself as a white witch. I have many women who come to me for help.' Elspeth explained

'What sort of help?'

'From health matters, to troubles of the heart, family problems, trouble with work colleagues and so forth. I make up potions. Some of the potions are from plants and herbs that I grow myself, others I buy over the internet.' Elspeth explained.

'And the hemlock?' Isabelle enquired.

'Hemlock is a poison but it is also curative in my experience. I have used it in small doses as a remedy for anxiety, for arthritis and asthma, even for someone suffering muscle spasms. Apparently it was used for whooping cough a long time ago. And I know before you lecture me on ethics, I know there is little scientific evidence for it but I have seen it work with my own eyes.'

'You grow it in your garden? My officers have seen it and we took an expert who identified it.' Isabelle stated.

'Yes of course. Its Latin name is Conium and it was and still is grown as an ornamental plant. As you have discovered, I grow it along the side of my land because it is beautiful but far enough away from any cows in the next field because it is poisonous to them if they ingest it.'

Elspeth looked at Isabelle and then at Quincy.

'So, you say that women come to you with their various problems and you try to help them?'

'That's right.'

'And Beatrice Gaultier was one such woman?'

'Yes, Beatrice Gautier was one of them. A very troubled woman. Her mother was also troubled. I guess modern medicine would describe it as a bipolar condition. Her mother would swing from depression to wild bouts of mania. She had over years hurt everyone around her, especially her daughter Beatrice. In the end her mother killed herself. Her father had fled years before because he could not cope. Scared more likely but he left his daughter as well, alone with her mother. Beatrice lived in fear of being the same. Apparently her grandmother was the same. Well, that is what she told me.' Elspeth explained and paused to sip her water.

'It was her hereditary nightmare - an ugly family heirloom, genetically encoded. Gifted down from generation to generation like a repeating time bomb, waiting for the clock to reach midnight. She was in constant fear that it would suddenly explode in her. The same bipolar medical condition. In her head, I guess it has shuffled, impatiently waiting and it fed her fear and uncertainty. She had married a man called Eric. I met him once. He seemed very mild mannered and he clearly adored her. I guess she was hoping that with him this mania would subside but it never did and instead it took its toll on both her and him and of course their marriage.' Elspeth explained.

Isabelle was uncertain where this was taking them but he continued to listen. Elspeth continued.

'Beatrice was never happy. But to be honest, it wasn't her unhappiness. It was her anger that was scary. She had told me some stories of what she had done when she was younger and her propensity for violence and unpleasantness. This did not sit comfortably with me. I was quite shocked and more than a little scared of her. But, she had sought help from me, so we tried many treatments and rituals to try to help her.'

'And did it?' Isabelle asked.

Elspeth looked a little awkward.

'Yes and no.' She replied.

Isabelle nodded for her to continue.

'One or two of the rituals involved some, what would I call it – theatrical punishment.'

'Theatrical punishment?' Isabelle repeated.

'Well, sort of being tied up and some light whipping.'

'OK' Isabelle responded.

'Nothing kinky, not sexual but more like a form of exorcism if you like. Being the person doing the..'

'Whipping' Isabelle tried to help her out with the words.

'Yes, suddenly she seemed different. Contented almost. It clearly fed a need or desire in her and when I saw her face, I admit I was more than a little worried.'

'Scared? Perturbed?' Isabelle encouraged.

'Yes. By then he had also taken a great interest in my knowledge and practice of herbalism and asked me many questions about it, how various herbs worked both on the body and on the brain. In many ways she became my prime student if you like'.

Elspeth sat back in her chair.

'Did this include hemlock?'

'Yes of course. It included everything', Shrugged Elspeth, ' But I also discovered that she had started a very passionate affair with another man. Her bouts of extreme happiness and depression seemed not to be genetic but about love and hate. Very quickly, she had become obsessed with this man, her secret lover and her anger within her had turned to poor old Eric. She would rant and rave about him. I became genuinely frightened. I felt somewhat responsible for what I was helping unleash.'

'I can imagine. What did you think she would do?' Isabelle enquired.

'Honestly, I don't know but I had my suspicions.'

'Which were?'

Elspeth shrugged helplessly.

'Do you think she could have started poisoning her husband?'

Elspeth sat there quietly and shrugged again, 'now that you are telling me that he was poisoned with hemlock then yes, I think that it was possible. I knew he had an illness but I never knew that hemlock was the cause. I guess I never asked because I never knew, never made the connection. Now you are asking me, yes, she knew how to make potions and so forth and as far as I knew, she did all the cooking at home.'

Again Elspeth took a sip of water and continued.

'Beatrice's mental state was becoming more extreme. Whether it was her affair with this unknown man or the marriage, or her genetic inheritance of her mother's and grandmother's condition, I just don't know. Then about a month before she disappeared she went cold.'

'What do you mean cold?'

'Cold. Emotionally dead. Not a depression but like a depression. Distant'.

There was silence in the room.

'When was this?' Isabelle asked, 'can you remember?'

'Oh I don't know. It was a long time ago. You'll need to help me,' she suggested.

'Eric told us that she disappeared early in the new year of 2011.'

'Yes that would fit, I couldn't tell you what year but it was after the winter solstice, sorry, Christmas time to you Christians.'

'Then what happened?'

'I never saw her again after she came to wish me well on the solstice. She just disappeared and never reappeared.'

'Have you seen her since?' Isabelle asked.

'No, never.'

Isabelle sat back and thanked her for her story.

'For the record' Isabelle then asked, 'are you saying that you never made her any potions or tinctures of hemlock?'

'Absolutely not. I had taught her many things but not how to make poisons.'

'How would she know then?'

'In our discussions and chats between her and I and others, we have always talked about the use of various herbs and plants throughout history from poultices to treatments, from hallucinogens to poisons and who used what and when. In terms of how to make any of these things, it is all there on the internet for anyone to read.'

Isabelle knew this to be true but she continued with her questioning.

'I know I asked you if you had seen her since and you said no but have you had any communication with her, letters, email, phone calls since the end of 2010?'

'None whatsoever,' Elspeth put her hand up to reiterate what she was saying, ' and for the record I would never teach anyone how to make out and out poisons. Some treatments could be considered harsh or extreme given the presenting problem but not to poison someone,'

'Or actual murder!,' Isabelle stated.

'What are you suggesting?' Elspeth looked shocked.

'Vincent Duvall was murdered on the 12th December 2010,' the Chief Inspector stated.

'So?' Elspeth asked

Vincent Duvall was poisoned and died from hemlock poisoning. Did you know who Beatrice was having an affair with?' Isabelle asked.

'No, she never said and to be honest, I did not want to know.'

'Are you sure it was not Vincent Duvall?'

Elspeth Brigande's face turned deathly pale. A mask of utter shock and horrible recognition has spread across her. It was clearly something that she had never considered, or as Isabelle noted later with Quincy, she was a very good actress.

'Oh my Gaia,' she muttered, 'oh no.'

They sat for a very long minute in silence but it was obvious that this conversation had gone as far as it could go. Chief Inspector Isabelle Dupont was satisfied with what Elspeth had been saying. Her story could very much be true. On the other hand it could be a good cover story or one where she was deflecting the blame.

Was Elspeth Brigande a serial poisoner and a murderer? At the moment she was in the frame with her personal connections but the evidence was far from clear cut.

Elspeth Brigande had behaved very differently to what Isabelle had expected from their first contact. Indeed, Isabelle had to accept that she too had come with some preconceived ideas about Elspeth. This had been a result of how the woman had been portrayed by others, coupled with her own stereotyping of what a white witch was, or looked like.

Indeed many healers and those skilled in medicine and nursing care had been condemned as witches across Europe in the middle ages and put to death or cast out of their communities. Most now practised, despite the internet, in a low key way to avoid ridicule or suspicion, or simply explained their work and interest in a more simple and esoteric manner.

However, Elspeth Brigande considered herself to be Alara the powerful and was an unusual character, somewhat bizarre who liked to engage in practices that were hard for most people to understand.

Isabelle was keeping an open mind but there was currently no good reason for not releasing her. Her next task was to track down Beatrice Gautier.

Isabelle thanked Elspeth Brigande for her help and explained that she was being released without charge but would need to be questioned further as the case progressed. Elspeth Brigande was clearly in shock. A terrible dawning had made her almost comatose and Quincy, who had sat mesmerised throughout the interview, was now trying to make arrangements for her to go home.

Isabelle went back to her office. She wrote herself some briefing notes and then telephoned Didier from her mobile phone.

'Didier' she said as he answered his phone, 'I hope you are well. I cannot go into details of the murder investigation but I thought that you should know, we had an anonymous tip off from someone about hemlock growing in a garden not too far from St Pierre. The tip off was very helpful and has helped the investigation. Naturally, I am sure that you do not have any idea who this person or persons are but should you hear anything through the usual tittle tattle and gossip of a village, please let it be known that it was very helpful.'

'I will indeed be Chief Inspector,' Didier had answered.

'Now, technically he, she or even they had been breaking the law. If they went onto the premises of the person where it was found. So they need to be careful. If they have any plans for further, how should I phrase it? Interventions, they need to be very careful. The case it seems has a new and potentially useful avenue of investigation, so we need to tread carefully.' Isabelle explained.

'Indeed Chief Inspector. I understand and will keep my ears and eyes open. Thank you for calling me and I wish you well in your investigations,' Didier then hung up and sat there in his kitchen smiling to himself.

Chief Inspector Isabelle Dupont was also pleased with this turn of events but now came the difficult part of turning such a lead into hard forensic evidence.

Chapter 21 – an award winning sausage

That evening, we were all invited to a special celebration outside the butcher's shop. Handsome Claude had now been awarded the top prize for Breton Sausages. This was not the first time that he had won it but for the last two years he had been in the final and only came second. He had held the prize for three years in a row before that and now he was back on top and was holding a celebratory BBQ cooking pork chops and his sausages with plenty of toasting with local cider, and wine.

'So Claude' Jean Paul shouted over the noise of everyone talking, 'now you have a prize sausage to go with your handsome good looks. How will you keep the women away?'

'I guess it won't be easy......hopefully' handsome Claude replied, smiling.

'My friend here', Jean Paul laughed and put his arm around Gerard, 'he has a prize sausage but thankfully he keeps it in his trousers' and laughed at his own joke.

Gerard smiled at Jean Paul.

'Did I tell you I have an old friend Cindy coming to visit me next month? You met her about five years ago when she was last here'. Gerard said.

'I remember her. Who could forget her? Beautiful and blonde and far too classy for you. I shall look forward to seeing her again'.

'And when you see her, do try not to stare and dribble this time, especially now you and Linda seem inseparable.'

Jean Paul put his glass down and looked seriously at his friend Gerard.

'Aaghhh, I've been meaning to tell you Gerard, Linda and I have been talking about getting married'. Jean Paul confessed.

'That was quick,' Gerard replied.

'Well we have known each other for nearly twenty years you know,' Jean Paul explained.

'Brilliant Jean Paul, I am pleased for you both'.

Any further conversation was interrupted with the arrival of Albert Jules, the Professor and myself.

'Good evening Professor', Gerard said and Jean Paul nodded along and then went and fetched two glasses of cider for the Professor and myself.

'Hey Professor, please don't be offended but how old are you?' Jean Paul asked.

Gerard and I bristled slightly. Albert Jules looked Jean Paul straight in the eye and said

'148 last birthday.'

The Professor held his gaze at Jean Paul.

Jean Paul, slightly taken aback, recovered quickly, 'I thought you must have been around that age from the old photos I've seen of you in this village.'

'How old are you Jean Paul?' Albert Jules returned the question.

'Not even close to being half your age – I'm 56.' Jean Paul replied.

'You look good for your age Jean Paul. Have you sampled one of Claude's sausages this evening?' He asked, changing the subject.

'No, not yet' Jean Paul said.

'Well, if you wouldn't mind, can you get me one in a galette while you are getting yours and go light on the mustard thank you.'

Then he turned to Gerard and myself

So, that answered Jean Paul's query about gentlemen my age. However, I suspect that he asked on behalf of you all?' and raised his cup of cider 'cheers' and he excused himself to go over and talk to the Mayor.

Gerard looked at me and smiled.

'That did indeed tell us, didn't it? He must have known that we had seen the photos that he was in. He is taking the piss, isn't he?'

I did not know. There were a number of things that I could not explain since I arrived here myself and sometimes it was difficult to remember everything that you do and experience over time and whether it is in all the right order. As I have said before I think I see the dead or certainly I sometimes see the living but they are from a different time. Who knows, maybe they are even from some parallel or alternative universe.

We are surrounded by granite in this village and the area around it and most of Brittany as a matter of fact. I once read a theory that our images can be transferred onto the stone in certain circumstances. Maybe that is what I see. More theories, more science and who knows. I should probably pluck up the courage to talk with Jean Paul about it. He was bound to have a favourite theory.

At the end of the day, they are what I see. I try not to talk about it because it scares other people or invites ridicule. I've never understood it beyond the fact that it is real to me. Albert Jules' age is just another one of those strange things that I have to confess that I do not understand. He could be 85 or 95 or as he said 148.

A complete mystery and did it really matter, even if it was possible.

Jean Paul returned with four prize winning sausages in galettes, handed one each to Gerard and myself and walked over to Albert Jules the Professor and handed him the sausage and galette and returned to us.

'He is taking the piss, isn't he?' Jean Paul asked us both. The very same question that Gerard had asked me I wanted to say - great minds think alike and fools never differ – but I chose not to and kept it to myself.

Instead we just bit into Claude's prize winning sausages and they were delicious.

In this village of the living and the dead or from another realm, my sense of reality had dimmed over time and what I had come to accept may just be my own reality.

But the so-called 'breeze' – now that was another matter.

Chapter 22 - Toulouse

Inspector Quincy Rochefort was forced to go and sit on the toilet and think, after he had finished talking with a doctor in Toulouse, early the next morning.

It was a conversation that as he was listening brought on the need to empty his bladder and rather unexpectedly, when he reached the toilet, his bowels also. This was a shock to him, especially as that was not his normal routine. The day had been quite normal in terms of his ablutions but after searching Elspeth Brigande's house, then the interview with her, he felt decidedly queasy. Then the conversation with the doctor in Toulouse had made him feel even worse.

He had been confused and not a little knotted up inside.

Having spent five minutes sitting on the toilet and completed the necessary proceedure for bladder and bowel. He felt what could only be described as a release followed by a surge of energy. He was onto something. He went and knocked on Chief Inspector Isabelle Dupont's door, opened it and walked in.

Isabelle beckoned him to sit down, which he did.

'I've just come off the telephone to a Doctor Richard Benoit down in Toulouse. He treated Beatrice Gautier in relation to the Carte Vitale expenses that we were tracing. It turns out that he was prescribing her a course of hormone treatments' Quincy explained,

'For her bipolar condition?' Isabelle enquired.

'No' Quincy replied excitedly, 'get this – she was having masculinising hormone therapy. She was being prescribed a low dose of testosterone, which they gradually increase over time.'

'Well,' was all Isabelle could say.

'The doctor treated her or should I say 'him to be' for six months then she/he never came back. I asked the doctor why not and he did not know. He wondered whether Beatrice changed her mind as the next steps would have been more radical.'

'More radical?' Isabelle asked

'Yes, if she'd chosen the next stage, then that involved the genitals and chest and bottom. I made the foolish mistake of asking what that involved, which I am sorry to say seems most unpleasant.'

Quincy Instantly felt the need to return to the toilet but suppressed the urge.

'Go on,' Isabelle urged.

Phalloplasty' Quincy said

'Is that what I think it means?' Isabelle asked

'Phalloplasty. They surgically make a penis from the female parts. It is all part and parcel of the transgendering process, apparently.'

'So what else do we have?'

'Well, we have an address for her through the carte vitale. But of course it is seven years old'.

'Get onto our colleagues in Toulouse and arrange for them to check the address out and to hold her for questioning if they find her', Isabelle instructed Quincy.

This he did, but not before he detoured back to the bathroom.

Despite the detour to the toilet, Quincy was remarkably efficient and within three hours, his colleagues in Toulouse went to the address they had for Beatrice Gautier.

The two officers, a man and a woman, knocked on the door which was answered by a middle aged man who introduced himself as David.

The officers explained that they were looking for Beatrice Gautier, who they understood either lived at this address or it was her last known address. David gave a knowing acknowledgement at the name and invited them in. They stepped into his kitchen and asked him who he was and he produced his identity card which had his photograph beside the name David Alarie.

David said that he had wondered who had lived there before him. He guessed that she must have been the previous tenant because when he moved in, some post arrived for her over the first few months but he had no forwarding address for her, so he posted them back to the postal service.

David wore spectacles, had black curly hair that was almost shoulder length and a black beard that was slightly greying.

He had asked if this Beatrice was OK or in some kind of trouble and should he do anything if he heard anything? The female officer handed him a card with her telephone number on it should he do so. They thanked him and left.

They returned to their car, drove to collect a baguette for their lunch. When they arrived back at their desks, they wrote up their incident reports for the morning including the visit to try to find Beatrice Gautier. That was their shift completed at 14.00 hours and went home to their respective houses.

So, the following day when they were back on duty they rang Inspector Quincy Rochefort with a report of their visit, explaining that she was no longer a tenant at that address, that mail had come for her but the new tenant had posted them back as he had no forwarding address.

It was after he had ended the call that he had a terrible feeling come over him. In the rush to try and track Beatrice Gautier down, he had not explained that Beatrice Gautier may no longer be a woman.

Quincy rang them back immediately and found himself talking to the female officer. He asked her to describe the current tenant, which she did, describing the man and his ID. He could understand why they did not think this was Beatrice.

'Did you take the new tenant's name?' Quincy asked.

'Yes of course. His name is David Alarie,' the female officer said and spelt it out for him.

Quincy reported his conversation with the officers to his boss, Isabelle Dupont. They both agreed that it was not a promising lead. But it was a lead nonetheless. He thought that Eric Gautier should be informed that his wife was still alive. Well she was seven years ago.

Quincy decided given the delicate nature of the treatment, that it was better to go and see Eric Gautier. Chief Inspector Isabelle Dupont agreed and said that she would accompany him.

When they arrived at Eric Gautier's house, Eric ushered them into his kitchen where they were seated at the table. Quincy did the talking and explained that they had had a lead from the use of the carte vitale. Eric had asked if she was OK and Quincy had had to explain how they had tracked her down and about the hormone treatment, as Eric was concerned it might have been something serious.

Quincy Rochefort tried to explain in the broadest of terms the treatment schedule. As far as Quincy was concerned, having a new penis created was pretty radical and pretty serious but he did not say anything. He kept the treatment detail as vague as possible in order not to distress the husband.

However, they needed to discuss with Eric, whether he had had any inkling into any of this.

Eric did not. This of course was a great shock to Eric. One listens to what you are being told and more often than not, does not take in all the details but some of the main parts of the conversation. What Eric took from the conversation, was that it was one thing for a wife to leave you but to have a wife that wants to become a man, well that was something else. Quincy had been as gentle as he could and he did offer Eric the opportunity to speak to him again once he had processed what he had just heard.

Quincy then explained that the officers had visited and there was a new tenant living there now who said that she had moved on but left no forwarding address.. Quincy then asked Eric whether he had ever heard of the current tenant – David Alarie. Eric had not.

They thanked Eric for his time and once in their car discussed the fact that it confirmed, firstly, that Beatrice was alive or had been. More importantly, it virtually confirmed that Eric had not murdered her when she had disappeared. This was key as it closed one line of enquiry that they no longer needed to follow. For Eric it helped dispel an accusation that he had had to live with for years.

Chapter 23 – Coincidence or what?

A few days later, Eric Gautier had taken Gerard out for a ride in his Bugatti. Eric did not have many friends. Gerard had been happy to join him. The car was a classic and with no windscreen on the passenger side the wind in his face, made the experience perfect. After forty minutes of driving around a whole lot of back roads, they decided to stop in the bar at La Croix de Bois, where of course I was sitting with Jean Paul and Linda.

They climbed out of the Bugatti and joined us just ahead of Didier who was strolling to the bar for what he called his kir o'clock drink (a kir and sparkling wine), which was usually five o'clock.

Once the drinks request had been conveyed to Marcel, the ever attentive bar owner, the conversation quickly turned to Eric and what he had found out from Inspector Rochefort.

There was an awkward silence between us all when he explained about the hormone treatment. There were very few husbands, whether their wife was with them or not, who would be happy that their wife wanted to become a man.

'Sounds like you've had a lucky escape there Eric,' Jean Paul said, 'it's one thing for some other man's penis to get in the way of your marriage but when its your wife with a penis, well that is a bit more unusual,' Jean Paul said pointing down at his crotch and looking for agreement with us all, 'Well that's more than a little alarming, isn't it?'

We all looked at Jean Paul and his ability to be so sensitive in difficult moments.

'Had you heard of the name of this new tenant, the Gendarmes met? No one from the past or connected to either of you?' Didier asked, putting his ex detectives head on and managing to change the conversation.

'Yes but it's a pretty common name. It was some guy called Alarie. His name was David Alarie, ' Eric stated.

'Oh my god' Jean Paul suddenly exclaimed, 'yes, it is a common name but do you know what it means – Alarie? It means – powerful. What a fucking coincidence! What are the chances of it? Oh fuck me',

'What Jean Paul are you going on about?' Linda asked.

Jean Paul threw his arms up wide.

'That women the white witch, the healer', he stammered

'What? Elspeth Brigande?' Gerard stated

'Yes, her. She called herself Alara, which means all powerful. Now what are the chances that Beatrice also gave herself a new name? Alarie, the male version, instead of Alara, and used it as her surname. I mean he. Oh whatever, he, she. Mister all powerful in Celtic, with his beard and what sounds like a wig hiding behind glasses. Have I gone completely mad it or am a fucking genius detective?'

Didier did not answer Jean Paul but pulled out his phone and rang Chief Inspector Isabelle Dupont immediately.

'I bet even those officers who went to the house were looking for a woman. They were not expecting a man with a beard, which I would put money on that was fake. The ID was obviously false and that threw them completely' Jean Paul had continued.

Didier had risen from his chair and walked to the end of the seating for quietness. When Jean Paul stopped talking we all turned to look at Didier still on the telephone. His call lasted a further five minutes and then he returned to us.

'They are going to go back to the apartment as a matter of urgency', Didier explained.

We then all turned, almost in unison to Eric Gautier, who was sat quietly listening to all this. He was deathly pale and staring into space.

'I'm sorry Eric, this must have been tough to hear over the last few days ' Didier said sympathetically.

Eric looked up at us all.

'What can I say? My wife has been missing for years. She was very possibly dead. In all that time, some people had me in the frame for it. Now, suddenly she is no longer dead, not even missing. She's been found but in that time, she has become a man. A man with a beard and glasses and a new name! Couldn't be easier to come to terms with – could it?'

'You certainly couldn't make it up,' Gerard replied.

'How close was Beatrice to this Elspeth? Didier asked.

Jean Paul was itching to say 'you mean David to Alara' but even he knew better than to say it.

'She spent a lot of time with her', Eric admitted, 'an increasing amount of time. I nearly said to her once or twice that I thought their relationship was bordering on an obsession but that's women for you. My experience is that they often have quite intense relationships over a short period of time and then it suddenly changes. Men seem to have longer term, less intense relationships. Maybe us men are just more shallow than women? I don't know but I have to admit the connection that Jean Paul has made is an interesting one and possibly correct.'

Eric shook his head 'I think we all need another drink. I certainly do'.

Chapter 24 – She's gone

One day later, Didier called us all together with a phone call to each of us, saying that he had news and that we all needed to hear it.

We sat down at the bar and Didier ordered a bottle of wine and five glasses. He waited until Maria came out with it on a tray and she filled the glasses. Didier took a sip and put the glass back down, to dramatic effect I have to say.

'Gone. Everything was gone.' he started. 'This David had left the flat and taken everything with him. I think that most likely, it wasn't a 'him', it was a 'her' – it must surely have been Beatrice. The Gendarmes went back yesterday evening. The landlord had no idea that she had gone or where she had gone. The ID turns out to be fake. There is no record of David Alarie anywhere.' Didier explained.

We all took our glasses and drank.

'So,' Jean Paul started, ' is he or she a woman or a man?'

'Clearly or unclearly, none of us know,' Gerard added.

The ex Inspector continued.

'The Chief Inspector has put out two alerts, one for Beatrice Gautier and one for David Alarie and is treating him or her as a likely murder suspect. What makes it harder, is that the only photos they had of Beatrice are old. In these photos, Beatrice has shoulder length hair. She clearly did not have shoulder length hair, when the Gendarmes visited her.'

'And a beard,' Jean Paul laughed, 'or possibly not now if it was false. Mind you, if it was real, then the hormone treatment must be working really well.'

Chapter 25 – Beatrice Gautier

Beatrice Gautier always thought that this day would come. She had gotten away with what she had done all those years ago but was wise enough to know that there was always a chance that what she had done could be uncovered. Then they would come looking for her.

This was why she had always kept a plan and an escape route that she could take within a couple of hours. She had never allowed herself to become complacent, even living as a man with a complete new identity. Now she was on the move and would have to change her identity again. She had done it once then she could easily do it again.

Someone somehow had linked her to the murder of that ridiculously vain man Vincent Duval. Did Duval deserve to die? Beatrice thought so then and thought so now. There was no remorse or regrets.

In her world he had jilted her after she had made so many sacrifices to him. She had poisoned her husband because Vincent did not want to share her with him. When she failed to poison him enough to kill him, he had simply abandoned her and that was something that she could not accept. It was her only weak spot – to try to kill her husband had been difficult because he was not a bad man and with hindsight she had not used enough hemlock.

What she had never understood was that Vincent Duval had not left her because she failed to kill her husband.

If the dead could talk then, Vincent Duval would have told her how scared he had become of her. How he tried to stop their affair because in a nutshell he had come to realise not just how mad she was but how dangerous. She had a penchant for being quite sadistic, could fly into a temper that appeared to have no rational explanation and could be violent towards him if he crossed her over matters that he often felt were trivial.

His happy fling with a married woman that was exciting and passionate had turned into an ugly and frightening relationship which he had tried to end but she had beaten him to it. She had tried to kill her husband and he had not tried to stop her. He had been too frightened.

The absolute horror, the sheer terror that passed through him as he realised that he was dying right in front of her. That he was dying of hemlock poisoning. He had been trapped in his own house by her and was unable to escape.

She had sat beside him, telling him what a sad and pathetic man he was, that he would soon lose bowel and bladder control as he died and that is how he was going to be found. She watched him fade away, eventually passing into unconsciousness and she quietly left in the darkness of the night.

For Beatrice it had been a surprisingly easy process to dabble around with hemlock poisoning to murder. She had become an expert on levels of the toxicity of hemlock. She had been experimenting for months to poison her husband.

Her desire for dominance and control had been with her from her teenage years with classmates and with a neighbour's son. That is when it had all started. The teenage neighbour had a simple crush on her and would do anything she asked. She had enjoyed degrading him and revelled in the power of her ability to control him in every way that she could.

How had it all come to this?

At school, Beatrice had gone from being a shy and lonely girl to a girl who frightened and intimidated her fellow classmates. For the first few years, when she was teased or picked on, she lived her retribution in her head. The nasty and vindictive thoughts she had stayed locked in her brain, until she was alone in her bedroom when her thoughts were spoken out aloud in an angry whisper. In her head she constructed unpleasant and vicious forms of torture and accidents to her classmates. Until one day, on the way home from school, another girl egged on by others taunted Beatrice about her short hair and her boyish shape.

Beatrice pushed her into the fountain in the park and held her head under the water while her anger and frustration poured out. She only stopped when she heard another girl screaming for her to stop. She pulled the girl out of the fountain and let her slide to the ground and then pointed her index finger at the other two girls who had been there egging her on to taunt Beatrice. They both turned and ran.

She was left alone by everyone in her class after that and the girl in the fountain had been too scared to report her. As a lonely girl and a lonely pupil the voices in her head grew steadily louder. Then about a year later Beatrice took action on another classmate, for no apparent reason other than this girl was very pretty and all the boys liked her.

Beatrice hid behind a tree with a long branch and waited for the pretty girl to cycle past the tree and she rammed the branch into the spokes of the bike, using the tree trunk as the buffer from the momentum of the bike. The wheel crumpled and the girl fell over the handlebars into the path.

Beatrice had hidden as soon as she struck the bike and so the girl never knew what happened properly because she had been looking the other way. As it happened, she was not badly injured beyond a grazed face and arms, plus a swollen ankle.

Beatrice had skipped merrily home, quite happy with what she had done. In fact she was not just quite happy, she was beside herself with pleasure and self satisfaction There was no remorse or guilt in her.

Beatrice knew that she was not a nice person and after she left school she worked in a supermarket. She took great pleasure in tampering with some of the fruit and vegetables with dirt and animal droppings and then watching customers buy them. Romantically she would go on dates with boys and ridicule them or tempt them into undressing and then leave and take their trousers and pants with her. Watching them trying to hide their nakedness or being seen by others was just so satisfying.

Sometimes she would completely lose her temper for no apparent reason. She lost her job at the supermarket because of her rage, punched the manager and then told everyone that he had tried to sexually molest her in his office.

Beatrice knew that part of her was out of control but had learned to compartmentalise her feelings and consequently her behaviour. The voices in her head were angry and demanded satisfaction.

She had systematically courted Eric because he was soft and compliant. Eric could give her some stability and sense of security. He was kind and timid. He loved and adored her and she knew that he felt blessed that she was with him. In return, he just wanted her to be happy.

Marrying him was the most logical thing that she could do. She could live a very simple double life. One in control of herself living with Eric, because he gave her the freedom to mostly do what she wanted to do. The rest of the time she could be wild and satisfy herself with whatever took her fancy whether it was pleasure or pain or exploring and pushing her own boundaries.

With Eric, she went into a sort of hibernation from her temper and evil and nasty thoughts and in that process considered herself to be the victim of others who had so enraged her in her life. But she could only keep this duality up for so long. The boundaries between the two were eroding, they were becoming blurred.

Then meeting up with Elspeth changed everything again. Elspeth, oh wonderful Elspeth, the white witch. This woman had introduced her to an avenue in which to explore the darker side of herself. To learn and understand her own desires and behaviours, to develop a valve for her anger and need to cause pain and suffering in others. It was to be life changing for Beatrice and even more life changing for some around her.

To start with, the chants and the rituals all seemed a bit theatrical but the women all seemed to possess an intensity that she knew that she had also. The mysticism was intriguing and she quickly realised that a couple of the women were more than a little strange. She had pondered that if she was a doctor then a psychiatric disorder would probably be easily applied to them. But Elspeth, or as she came to know her, Alara, was indeed a powerful lady. Her knowledge of herbs and plants as ingredients for healing as medicine and as poultices and oils for the skin and even as combating things like anxiety, was impressive.

However, it was a ritual that she was invited to join with Alara at a house an hour's drive away that changed everything for her. Halfway through the evening, the ritual began. It was January and the room they were in had a roaring open fire, some wine that had been blessed had been taken and a man and a woman were tied with soft material around their wrists to one another and Alara produced a scourge (the whip) and struck them both on their naked buttocks.

This started to arouse Beatrice. Then to her utter dismay, Alara handed her the scourge and told Beatrice to strike them each and to do it three times. Beatrice was timid with the first stroke each but the couple did not cry out in pain nor asked for forgiveness. With the second two strokes, she had found herself giddy with arousal. The room was hot and the strong smell of oils being burnt seemed to increase the intensity.

On the third stroke she was in some kind of ecstasy and almost a frenzy. Alara took her hand and asked her for the whip back sensing how Beatrice felt. Another woman in the room untied the couple and they all hugged one another. Beatrice did not know what to do and sat down in one of the armchairs, while the couple dressed in front of her.

Alara stood by her and stroked Beatrice's head. It was as if something had shifted in her head. Beatrice had enjoyed inflicting pain on this couple who had seemed to be more than happy to let it happen.

Beatrice did not understand the ritual but was sure Alara would explain it to her at some stage. Beatrice however, realised that she did not really care for an explanation. It was the pleasure that came with the release in her head that mattered for Beatrice.

She became an avid follower of Alara and learnt more and more about white magic as Alara described it, and about herbalism and what was medicinal and curative and what was poison.

Beatrice now had an open and legitimate way in which to satisfy herself and feed her anger with the world, rather than committing random acts. She started to attend gatherings away from Beatrice where she met more troubled souls, people who were equally happy to explore their own darker sides and with Beatrice.

The problem for Beatrice and poor Eric was that she began to realise that she no longer needed him to be her safety net. She had felt a release and from being her stabilising rock. Eric had become the anchor tying her down. She had grown to despise him. No matter how unpleasant she was to him, he would simply smile and try to hide how wounded he felt and then try even harder to keep the peace and tell her how much he loved her.

So Beatrice started to explore ways that would bring their relationship to an end and what she had learnt about herbs and plants and particularly hemlock. To start with she applied small amounts in his meals, which was easy to do in stews and chilli con carne and he started to become unwell. With him unwell and at home because he was not able sometimes to go to work, it backfired on her as she could not go out as much.

Even worse, with him looking ill and pitiful, she felt an anger and frustration grow in her with him. The fact that she was causing this never connected in her head. As he grew more unwell the more she wanted to hurt him.

On top of that she had met and started seeing Vincent Duval. It was a new and passionate relationship and she seemed to want very little apart from sex. She knew that he was delighted to engage in whatever she fancied to start with and then demanded. Her needs and desires were more than a little on the sadistic side for his liking but he let her. It was something new and exciting for Vincent at the beginning. For Beatrice that was all that mattered.

Meanwhile on the domestic front, it finally came to the point where she started to administer a higher dose in Eric's food and he was hospitalised.

No sooner had she hospitalised her husband, then that bastard Vincent Duval started to get cold feet about their relationship and was becoming scared of her demands. So she decided to finish their relationship. Beatrice considered the options. The fairest and most logical way, was to poison him and so she did with hemlock. No one knew about their relationship, least of all her husband Eric.

She had planned it all meticulously, poisoned him and had simply disappeared, leaving no trace of where she had gone.

Now she was on the run and was very angry. She had never gone through with the surgery. The hormone therapy had started to create changes to her body but so had it increased her feeling of anger and aggression. She also realised that such treatment was one way that she could in theory be tracked down. So she had stopped the treatment. Instead, she had simply dressed as a man and acquired a new ID. Doing this had not been easy, nor cheap but it had been worth it.

None of it was perfect but it had worked and it had certainly fooled the two gendarmes who had come looking for Beatrice Gautier.

The last few years alone, she had retreated back into her own thoughts and introspection. The voices in her head were loud and becoming louder. There was only one realistic outcome.

That outcome was to destroy any remaining evidence that linked him to her past. Two witnesses who would need to be silenced – The first was Elspeth Brigande, the white witch. With her gone, any link to her past was ended. Beatrice could then start a new life. She could become Alara the powerful and replace her former mentor. The second witness was poor old Eric, her husband who she should have poisoned properly instead of experimenting with the doses of hemlock in his stews.

What she needed to do is have Elspeth Brigande appear to have poisoned poor old Eric, who when he realised that he had been poisoned kills the intolerable white witch. In that way, if she was arrested then she could possibly explain the lengths that she had had to go to protect herself from the evil Elspeth Brigande by disappearing for so long.

Chapter 26 – The Professor

I received an unexpected telephone call from a ward nurse at the hospital. The duty doctor was concerned about Albert Jules. Albert Jules had collapsed outside of his house and been rushed to hospital the day before. He was asking if we could go and see him. When I mean 'we' it was Gerard, Jean Paul and myself.

When we arrived we told the nurse who we were. She explained that Albert had not broken any bones, was conscious but was extremely tired. His blood pressure was low and it was worrying them. She asked us how well we knew him. Has he been suffering with any illnesses lately? Had he been having trouble sleeping or eating?

As far as we were aware he had been in reasonable health, considering his age. She looked at us all and smiled.

'I think that you have arrived at an important time for him to talk with you,' she said knowingly

When we entered his room we were confronted by Albert sitting slightly propped up on pillows. He did look frail and very tired, in stark contrast to the last time we had seen him about a week ago.

'My friends' he greeted us and a smile spread across his face, 'thank you for coming to see me'.

As usual with hospital rooms there was only one chair. Jean Paul took the chair, Gerard sat on the side of the bed and I remained standing by the window.

' What happened to you Professor?' Jean Paul asked.

'I collapsed outside my house. Nothing more dramatic than that.

Thankfully the neighbour saw me and called the paramedics straight away and here I am.' old Albert explained.

'And here you are,' Gerard repeated and rubbed the Professor's shoulder. Albert then held out his arm and took Gerard's hand into his.

'Please do not be alarmed at what I have to say to you. Some of what I want to say will make sense and some of it won't. I am a very old man, I am tired and I know my time to depart this world has finally come,' he said quietly. We all sat and in my case stood there in silence.

The Professor continued.

'I have spent so many years watching over this village. So many years that I can no longer remember exactly. I have tried to protect it as best as I can. I have tried to encourage local souls, like yourselves and some before your time, to come to decisions, to take action, that keep the village thriving and safe. Now, it is time to hand the baton over,' and he squeezed Gerard's hand,' and who better than you Gerard, with your two good friends to support you, to take on this role.'

Albert stretched to get his glass of water, beside the bed, which had a straw in it and Gerard passed it to him and held it for him while the Professor sucked on the straw through two dry looking lips. When he had finished, Gerard put the glass back down on the cabinet and with that Albert lay back on his pillows.

'There are things that I have seen that are hard to explain and to understand.' He said and then turned to Jean Paul.

'I know you think that I am some kind of wizard or something like that, Jean Paul. You have a wonderful creative mind tucked inside a formidable knowledge of facts, information and of course ridiculous tittle tattle. To be blunt, many villagers think it is all drivel and foolish stories but my dear boy, don't you ever change. You are a collector and procurer of history and facts.'

Then he smiled to himself 'And Jean Paul, with that unusual mix, I know that you are curious to find out whether I told you the truth. Am I really 148 years old? Of course, logic tells you that that is impossible but somewhere in that head of yours you believe that it could just possibly be true. You think it might just be possible because you and your friends have seen things in this village that are hard to explain.'

'And all the photos sort of make sense if you are that old' Jean Paul smiled.

The Professor smiled at himself and raised his hand slightly, 'Photos, internet, records, clocks. Our lives become more complicated with modern technology. Wonderfully helpful on the one hand and highly problematic on the other.'

'Like being 148 and no one can believe it?' Jean Paul interrupted.

'Jean Paul, we are ruled by the desire to log everything and to record everything. Everything has to be measured down from decades, to years and days, and even down to minutes and seconds. Be happy with what we are blessed with that you can see with your own eyes and smell with your nose. We have perfectly constructed sets of seasons. The sun arrives every morning and then sets in the evening, even if it is cloudy or raining. The house martins retire at dusk and then the bats take over with their shift. Our bodies should be in tune with all these rhythms of life.'

I could see Jean Paul listening and acknowledging what the Professor was saying whilst at the same time realising that he was not going to get a definitive answer.

'Over time your knowledge, Jean Paul, will be indispensable for this village. The fact that you cannot just accept that there are photographs of my past relatives, who lived here in La Croix de Bois. Why should I not look exactly like my dead grandfather or great uncle? You are blessed and cursed, at the same time, with an active and curious mind. It makes you think differently and sometimes, as they say outside of the box. Sometimes you think the near impossible and sometimes the near impossible could be true and if not true then worth exploring in order to gain further insight.'

'Your talent will be indispensable to your good friend Gerard who will take over my mantle of what should we call it? Unofficial watcher of La Croix de Bois? But I was talking of the rhythms of life, and mine is just about over.'

He squeezed Gerard's hand again and with that, smiled and said 'Bon Courage.' He closed his eyes and his face froze. He just stopped breathing, his smile on his face, looking serene

The three of us stayed very still and looked at this frail old man on the bed. I do not know what we expected, some kind of shaft of light or to see his spectral spirit lifting above him from his bed and physical body. It was certainly a strange moment. Dear old Professor Albert Jules had simply passed away in front of us.

One moment he was talking softly and coherently and then suddenly he had ceased to exist and had left us. He transformed from a tired old man who nonetheless was vibrant, the next he was gone, leaving just a frail carcass of a body lying on the bed; recognisable in his form but in another sense not so.

John Paul stood up and went over to the window and opened it.

He turned to Gerard and myself.

'Just letting his spirit out' he shrugged..

Gerard was deep in thought and had not moved, still holding Albert's hand in his.

Jean Paul returned to the bed and sat on it.

'Bloody hell Albert,' Jean Paul muttered, 'thanks a lot. You just leave us eh? As per usual, yet more questions and riddles for us rather than answers.'

We all looked at one another and sat there in silence for a further five minutes before we went and spoke with the nurse. The three of us needed to go and get a coffee and talk about what he had said to us. Albert had been coherent when he was talking to us but had also rambled that had left us equally confused between some sort of vague understanding of what he was saying and complete nonsense.

' Will you still be taking sugar in your coffee, now you are an unofficial watcher of La Croix de Bois?' Jean Paul asked Gerard as he passed him a coffee from the drinks machine.

As we sat drinking our coffee in the visitor's area in the hospital, unknown to us, events around us were unfolding with great haste and we would have little time for contemplation in the next few days.

Chapter 27 – Back to the 'coven'

Beatrice Gautier woke up in her van. She had turned off the motorway between Nantes and Rennes, into a parking and picnic area. In her van was her sleeping bag, water and some food, clothes, gloves and an array of tools, plastic fasteners, tape, blankets and rope, a set of locksmith keys and two bottles of chloroform. Her other belongings she had left in what she called her latest safe house, a holiday home belonging to an Irish couple, one of whom was now in a care home back in Ireland, so no-one was due to travel there for the foreseeable future.

The chloroform she had acquired a couple of years ago. She had met with a man. A complete stranger, who thought he was in with a chance with him as David, especially as he was armed with the chloroform. As he tried to apply the chloroform over his mouth, the wig had come loose and fallen off. In his shock, he had been too slow to react and David Alarie had been too quick for him. He had suddenly found the cloth over his own mouth and it was he who passed out.

Waking up and tied up and someone laughing at him was bad enough. Then he discovered that David was still actually a woman, which was surprising enough. But when he started to understand that she was also a violent psychopath, who took great delight in torturing him, his fear took hold. Faced with this and unable to move, the fact that she robbed him of his wallet and his bank card details felt like a relief in comparison.

Another perfect crime really. This man was never going to report what had happened and of course Beatrice had been careful to only remove 500 euros from the account, which on top of the 450 he had in his wallet was not a bad evening's work. Lastly, he was made very aware that this bisexual, transexual, mad man or woman had his address and personal details.

So chloroform, although not as potent as the TV shows and films would have you believe but a decent dose could render someone unconscious for between 20 minutes and 2 hours depending on how concentrated the dose was. The secret was to either overpower the victim or ideally incapacitate them first so a stronger dose can be held in place over the airways.

Beatrice knew that it would come in useful, somewhere down the line.

Beatrice had spent the last 24 hours going over and over in her head what she planned to do and how to do it. In her mind she searched through the different options and the possible pitfalls and mistakes that could happen. In this way, she eliminated as many of the risks as possible.

The logical planning and processing was never quite as exciting as the chances that present themselves out of nowhere, as it had been with the latest 'squeeze.' Through the carefully planned ones were ultimately the most satisfying as they reached fruition. The planned one's also allowed her to control her emotions and it was this control that had kept her hidden and safe for these last few years.

She drank some water out of a bottle and ate a cheese and ham baguette in the driving seat of her van. She knew she should never get hungry in case she had to adapt her plans. She then went to the toilets in the parking area and to check herself out that she looked as nondescript as possible.

On her way back she checked the van for any obvious faults or problems. The last thing she needed was to be pulled over by any zealous gendarme. She joined the motorway to Rennes and on to her intended targets driving at a steady 100 kilometres an hour where the speed limit was 110.

Her first strike would be at Elspeth Brigande's house. The white witch's house was easy. It was isolated and unless someone was visiting, then there was little or no risk to her being seen. Even so, she would take the time to stake out Elspeth Brigande. She could leave the van quite near the house without being seen and approach it on foot. Her tools of the trade would be in one bag. The woman had no pets or not when she knew her, and she doubted that had changed but of course she would look for clues first.

Eric's house should be equally easy. She still had the keys to the house. Had he changed the front and back door locks? She doubted it but it would not matter. Breaking into houses and flats had become an easy occupation for her over the years but having the keys certainly made life a lot easier.

She also knew that she could park the van right behind the house on an old dirt track that only the farmer used and that would be in the daytime. There were trees and bushes between the track and the house.

Chapter 28 – A marriage proposal

Jean Paul had asked whether Gerard or myself could take him for his hospital appointment. He was due to have an operation on a hernia. It was a minor proceedure which would involve being a day patient. It was agreed that I would take him and Gerard would collect him.

Linda was working late that day, which is why Gerard was collecting him. The likelihood of Linda being up never mind awake at 6.30 in the morning was not even worth contemplating, hence I was driving him there.

The operation went very well but it seemed to have a double impact on Jean Paul. It was the meaning of life for him. All the way home with Gerard, Jean Paul had kept talking about when the general anaesthetic was put in his body he ceased to exist in that moment. Nothing, no conscious thought, no dreams. He kept on talking about understanding the utter nothingness. He equated it to being like death. You simply cease to exist. You have no worries about paying the electricity bill or a hangover, or what the meaning of life was all about. The fact that the universe was likely to cease to exist in 13 billion years, would no longer trouble him.

'It's like going to sleep' Gerard suggested, as he had had a general anaesthetic three times in his life.

Jean Paul had gone home and gone to bed and had been told to take it carefully for a few days and not lift heavy things for the next few weeks, which suited Jean Paul very much. He had

Linda to look after him.

The next evening, we both called around to see him and he was even more perplexed,

'Listen boys' he started, ' having a general anaesthetic is nothing like going to sleep. Apparently, during sleep, the brain moves between the slow and fast waves. The slow waves are the non REM sleep and the fast the REM sleep. When you are under, our brain waves are sort of tied up or held hostage and stay like that throughout the operation. We're in a sort of suspended state.'

We sat there looking at him.

'And even more weirdly, at exactly the same time I ceased to exist, Linda woke up at 09.30 with a start. Linda has never woken up before 10.00 and rarely before 10.30. How about that for a coincidence?'

'Soul mates' Gerard said.

'Exactly. Which brings me to my final thing to tell you.' and he shouted to Linda to come in and join us.

'I know that I was bending your ear Gerard about thinking about proposing to Linda. So after this operation and for us to share such a coincidence, it was the icing on the cake so to speak, Jean Paul explained.

'Not the chantilly cream on the old man, ' Gerard laughed, reminding him of a previous conversation that had been had.

'No, Linda and I have been friends for so long and the last few weeks have been magical. Linda and I have decided to get married. I proposed to her and she said YES. Now I, sorry, I mean we would like you both to be best man. Would you agree to that?'

We both looked at them and said that we would be delighted, knowing such a union would have ramifications that would invade all our lives for evermore. Good ramifications.

Once again that 'breeze' had woven something.

Chapter 29 – Taken alive

Eric Gautier was unceremoniously dragged out of the car by his feet and then dumped onto the ground on his back, his hands still tied together in front of him with plastic strip fasteners.

As he meandered into some form of consciousness, he felt groggy and nauseous. He did not know how long he had been unconscious. He was uncertain where he was.

As his head cleared he became aware of another body trussed up about five metres away. At first he did not recognise who it was. He dreamingly noticed the mass of hair and wild eyes and thought that he had seen these features before. As his vision cleared those same features registered as belonging to none other than Elspeth Brigande, firmly tied up and in a writhing fury against her bonds.

Slowly, what had happened to Eric came back to him. Eric remembered a noise behind him, when he was sitting in his kitchen earlier, eating toast. His radio had been on and he was listening to a tiresome debate between a right and left wing politician whose sole point of agreement was how much they detested the President. The next moment he caught a movement to the right of his head and that was all. Now he was tied up next to a white witch, who seemed demonic. He had no idea how long he had been unconscious but his head was throbbing and it felt sore but his restraints would not allow him to check for damage.

Elspeth Brigande recognised the face of Eric Gautier, but no name to her to match the face. She did not know what had happened nor who had tied her up. One minute she had been lying in bed dozing until a hooded and masked intruder had smothered her mouth and lay across her whole body. The cloth across her mouth and nose had a slightly sweet smell and her brain thought it smelled of hospitals. She struggled to stay conscious and then her ability to move the weight on top of her became impossible and she felt her world drifting slowly away and drowsiness beginning to overpower her.

When she gained consciousness, she had no idea what had happened nor the time span and she seemed alone in her living room, tied by her ankles and by her knees and her wrists tightly bound behind her back. She had tape across her mouth.

She had been conscious for a while when she heard the door open and saw a man being dragged into the lounge by his ankles by someone dressed in a hoodie and mask, which she assumed was her abductor. He was tied up the same way as she was and as he was placed next to her on the floor.

Then with a sudden sense of realisation, she not only recognised him but could put a name to him. It was Eric Gautier, the husband or ex husband of Beatrice Gautier. She had only met him once and seen him from a distance but there could be no mistake.

It was then that a sense of dread overcame her. This sense of dread was heightened when her assailant removed her mask and let down her hoodie. It was the face of Beatrice Gautier. In one sense she had not changed one bit. Her hair was cut much shorter and it was a different lighter colour. It was the eyes that she instantly recognised, a dark brown and an intensity to them that bore down on her. Penetrating eyes that did not blink.

Many people would look into those eyes and immediately look away, for they were the eyes of a mad person. But not Elspeth Brigande. She held that stare in an equally manic and angry manner. Her student, her understudy was leaning over her and had tied her up.

She had felt the dread surge through her and then fought it. How dare this monster cause her so much trouble and so much pain. Whether it was the last thing that she would do, she would make Beatrice Gautier suffer. She knew equally that Beatrice Gautier intended the same fate for her.

Chapter 30 – Gerard takes control

Gerard woke up early and made himself a coffee and decided that with everything that was happening then he should go and pay Eric a call to see how he was doing. He finished his coffee and drove over to St Pierre. He knocked on Eric's door and in doing so realised that it had not been shut properly and creaked slightly open.

'Eric' he shouted and knocked again, this time more loudly. He heard no response, so opened the door fully and stepped inside and what he saw immediately worried him – an armchair was turned on its back. There was glass on the floor and there was liquid spread across the rug that was by the chair. It looked like a drink that had been spilled.

'Eric' Gerard called, 'Eric, are you in? Are you OK?'

There was still no response. Nothing, just the ticking of his grandfather clock by the door into the kitchen. Gerard walked into the kitchen and looked out into the garden. Eric was not there and the back door was unlocked. He turned and went to the stairs where he cautiously took one step at a time until he reached the landing and then went into the two bedrooms, looked in the toilet and then in the bathroom.

There was no Eric. Gerard walked back down the stairs and out into the garage. Again the door was unlocked but inside was his treasured Bugatti. This troubled Gerard and he took out his telephone and rang Didier, who answered after it rang twice.

'Didier, I'm at Eric's house and there is no sign of Eric and it looks like there has been an accident or a struggle in the living room with his armchair overturned and a spilled drink on the rug. The Bugatti is parked outside but there is absolutely no sign of him.'

Didier thought for a minute and then replied

'Gerard, stay there and try and look to see if his phone is there. I'm going to ring Inspector Rochefort and tell him what you've found and I would imagine that he will come over to look at the scene'.

'OK' Gerard replied and cut the call and began searching for a mobile phone. When he looked around the other side of the chair, what he saw disturbed him even more. There was blood on the side of the chair and underneath the chair a hammer with blood on it.

He then rang Eric's mobile phone. He heard it ringing in the room that he was standing in. He sat the armchair up and found it jammed down the side between the arm of the chair and the cushion.

He tried to ring Didier back but the phone was engaged. It was engaged because Didier was trying to reach the Inspector, but with no luck. The reason for this was because Inspector Quincy Rochefort was at that moment sitting on the toilet seat in the Gendarmerie. It was nine fifteen and Quincy's best work was done once he had finished his daily bowel evacuation. Like everything else in Quincy's life, he was thorough and followed routine's long established routine, so even if he did not feel the urge to go to the toilet, this is what he always did once he was at work.

So in reality it was rarely an in and out job and would take some time. So his phone lay on his office desk buzzing away whilst his bowels remained stubbornly closed.

Gerard tried Didier twice at exactly the same time that Didier was trying the Inspector.

With everything that Gerard knew about the case and the situation he was looking at, he felt he had to do something. He went to the house next door and knocked at it and Eric's neighbour answered.

'I'm looking for Eric. Have you seen him or heard him?'

'Not today,' the neighbour answered.

'Any visitors?'

'No'

'Ambulance?'

'No nothing – is he OK?' the neighbour asked, looking worried.

Gerard looked around and across the gardens.

'What's behind the hedge and trees at the back of the garden?' He asked.

'An old track that the farmer uses. Why?'

Gerard thanked him and ran over to look at the track which was only about 15 metres from the house. He noticed that it then bent around the third garden and joined the road about 50 metres further down. A vehicle could easily have been parked right by Eric's house without anyone noticing.

He looked at the ground and some of the grass and wildflowers had been flattened. He realised that he could be jumping to conclusions as the neighbour had said that the farmer used the track but these looked like van tracks rather than those of a tractor.

Gerard ran back to his car – what to do? He rang Didier again and this time his call connected. He told Didier, as calmly as he could, his heart hammering in his chest, that on a hunch he was going to drive over to Elspeth Brigandes house to check if Eric, for some reason, was there. He could not think of anything nor anywhere else that Eric could be. He told Didier to keep trying Inspector Rochefort. He then rang me and I agreed to meet him over at the house of the white witch.

Gerard jumped into his car and sped off. Elspeth Brigande's house was about two kilometres outside of the village of St Pierre. He was there in under five minutes and slew his car to a halt in front of the house besides two other vehicles, one a car and the second a van. He ran to the door and banged on it. There was no reply. He banged again and there was still no answer. Yet there were two vehicles already in the drive, so someone had to be in. He looked at the vehicles and felt the bonnets of both. The van's bonnet was still slightly warm.

He went to the window of the kitchen but could not see anyone. He tried the kitchen door but it was locked. He went around the side of the house and looked through the window into the lounge. He thought that he could see some movement from behind the sofa and peered closer through the window.

Suddenly in front of him, he saw something coming towards the window being swung right at him. He instinctively tried to duck down. The window exploded into pieces of glass that showered his head and shoulders and a sharp object came through where the glass had been. The impact and shock sent him reeling back and he toppled over onto the ground. As he looked up he saw what that sharp object was. It was an axe blade and shaft that had come through the glass. It was being held by a woman, who looked very much like Eric's wife, Beatrice.

'Fuck off and stop bothering us,' she cursed at Gerard. 'You're trespassing. This is private property.'

Gerard climbed to his feet and looked at her. He went back around to the kitchen door, which looked much flimsier than the old oak front door. He quickly scanned around the garden and the sheds and spotted an old spade, propped against a wall. He picked it up and ran to the door. In his head, he knew that he should probably wait until the Gendarmes arrived but having an axe aimed at you, coming through a window was not a normal reaction nor response to knocking on a door.

A spade was not the best for opening a locked door but he thrust the spade between the door and the frame as he knew this would be the weakest part. After four thrusts with the spade, it was making a purchase into the gap. He could see that it was starting to open between the frame and door. He thrust the spade in between the door and frame again but this time, used the handle as a lever. He pushed with all his weight and suddenly the door gave way, causing him to lose his balance.

As the door opened Beatrice Gautier flew out, axe in hand.

'Fucking bastard, I'm going to fucking kill you' she screamed and swung the axe at Gerard, who simply rolled away and half climbed to a squat as she ran at him again with the axe. This time, Gerard sprang forward and hit her with his right shoulder into her thighs and she fell backwards.

Gerard climbed to his feet and walked towards Beatrice as she also stood up. The axe was still in her hand.

'Fuck you' she said again and went to lift the axe.

Gerard stepped forward and for the first time in his life, he hit a woman. A straight punch to the mouth and nose. Beatrice fell backwards.

'No, fuck you instead' he said softly and looked at her. She was conscious but not moving much and blood was pouring from her nose.

'Sorry Dad' he muttered to the sky as he stepped over her and picked up the axe and threw it as far away as he could. His father had bought Gerard up to always be courteous to women, open doors for them, listen to them, let them always have the last word in any argument and no matter how much they wound you up, never, ever hit a woman. He had done exactly that throughout his entire life until this moment.

Gerard ran inside calling out for Eric. In his panic and adrenaline filled head he had completely forgotten the name of the white witch but still had the good sense not to call out, 'are you there white witch?'

He ran behind the sofa and there to his utter relief was Eric and the white witch alive but bound by the legs and ankles and hands with tape over their mouths. He pulled the tape from Eric's mouth and then he took off the tape across Elspeth's mouth and as he did so, her name jumped into his head. He ran back to the kitchen and came back with a knife to cut the plastic ties on Eric's hands and gave him the knife to continue to untie himself and Elspeth.

Gerard went back outside to check on Beatrice, who was now on her knees, cursing and trying to get up. He stood over her, a little unsure what to do. He could not hit her again but he was certain that she was in no mood for a conversation.

Suddenly, he was shoved to one side by the bustling white witch. Beatrice had just got to her feet, when Elspeth Brigande lunged herself full on at her. Beatrice fell backwards into the ground and Elspeth landed on top of her. Her knees pinned Beatrice to the ground. She then slapped her very hard across the face. That answered Gerard's dilemma on what was best to do.

'That'll teach the bitch,' she spat.

Elspeth then stood up over the prone body of Beatrice. She looked like she was ready for further retribution.

'We need something to tie her up,' Gerard said as calmly as he could. He could feel his heart still hammering in his chest.

'Go and get the rest of the ties she was using,' Elspeth said, 'I've got this fucker covered,' Gerard turned back into the house and within a minute came back and tied her up by the wrists and ankles.

Gerard turned around and Eric was standing by the splintered door frame holding his blood encrusted head.

'How are you doing Eric?' Gerard asked.

'A lot better than I was about ten minutes ago when she had that knife ready to plunge into me.'

'Your timing could not have been better,' Elspeth said to Gerard and then continued,' You look vaguely familiar but who are you?' She asked.

'Gerard. I live in La Croix de Bois.'

In the distance they could hear sirens. I arrived just before the Gendarmes. Too late to be of any use but at least I was there. I went straight over to inspect Eric's head wound and then the Gendarmes and Inspector Quincy Rochefort arrived.

All of them looked shocked to see a woman who was barely conscious, tied up on the ground, a man with a bleeding head wound and a wild wild looking woman her hair bedraggled standing like a statue of an Amazonian warrior cursing and mumbling a chant like torrent of incomprehensible words.

Gendarme training had never prepared them for such a sight and it was Gerard who had to tell Inspector Rochefort who to arrest and who to attend to, although if the truth be known it was the person due for arrest who looked in the worst state.

Chapter 31 – A murderous explanation

What to say?

Beatrice Gautier was arrested and taken away. She was charged with the murder of Vincent Duval, the attempted murder of her husband Eric and the kidnapping and assault of both her husband Eric and Elspeth Brigande. It was highly likely that Beatrice intended to murder both Eric and Elspeth. Gerard's timely arrival had thankfully stopped that happening. When Gerard had arrived, the knife was being held to Eric's chest and his knocking on the door had stopped her from plunging the knife into his chest.

Like too many crazy people, Beatrice had gone into a long monologue that was vile and vitriolic but measured, in a very cold and analytical way.

Gerard had arrived, not a moment too soon as she had systematically explained what was going to happen to Eric and Elspeth, how they would suffer at her hands and how the evidence would look once they were both dead.

Beatrice explained that when she walked out after killing them both, the evidence would be clear. The evidence would demonstrate that Elspeth, the white witch, had killed Eric before taking her own life in utter despair. Elspeth, who had always had a crush on Beatrice, had systematically poisoned Beatrice's husband Eric, so that she could be with Beatrice. Luckily for Eric, Elspeth had not used enough hemlock to kill him with. When she had discovered that Beatrice had taken a lover instead and was having an affair with Vincent Duval, then Elspeth Brigande had simply poisoned the poor man with a much bigger and lethal dose of hemlock.

Fearing for her own life, Beatrice had had no option but to flee for her own safety from a murderous Elspeth Brigande. That life had to be one of going into hiding and changing her name and identity. She could not even tell her husband. She could not even report Elspeth because she had no proof then.

Elspeth had never managed to find Beatrice. Why Elspeth had decided to turn on Eric and kill him, after all this time, Beatrice could not explain. Beatrice thought and hoped that by staying out of contact with Eric, she had been able to keep him safe. This was at great personal and emotional cost to her. This was the only way to keep her safe and Eric safe from this monster of a white witch. She could only shrug to the Gendarmes that something must have happened to change all that but did not know what that was.

She was heartbroken for her estranged husband Eric and utterly relieved that Elspeth Brigande was no longer amongst the living. Her only consolation was that she could now come out of hiding and resume some form of normal life.

When she had finished, she let out a long sigh.

Then Beatrice told them how they were going to die, but before they died, how they were both going to suffer at her hands. This is when they heard the arrival of the motor car that Gerard was in.

The evidence the Inspectors had for the killing of Vincent Duval was still no more than the hemlock poisoning. The confession of what Beatrice Gautier had done to Vincent Duval and what she planned to do to Eric and to Elspeth, once the investigation had been concluded, would, they hoped, be strongly taken into account by the presiding judge. Whether Beatrice confessed later under interview or in court to all this, the Inspectors were hopeful, coupled with the kidnapping and attempted murder of Eric and Elspeth, that they were looking at a conviction for a sentence of many years, if not life in prison.

Chapter 32 – A final revelation....or not?

After all the excitement, Eric invited us all to eat at one of the local restaurants to thank us all for our help and especially for Gerard, who had probably saved his life along with Elspeth Brigande's life.

Gerard had brought along his very good friend, Cindy, who had come to visit him for the weekend. Like Gerard, she was in her late fifties and age had not allowed her to lose her natural beauty nor her shape, which we all noticed, including Linda. Put simply, Cindy was stunning.

Cindy and Gerard had been friends for 35 years but he had never talked about her much apart from how long their friendship had lasted and how much they cared for one another. So Jean Paul was not going to lose this opportunity. Gerard had been married but his wife had passed away when they were both in their forties through cancer. His two children, Maria and Olivier now both lived in Paris and both of them were married. Gerard had stayed friends with Cindy throughout his marriage.

Jean Paul turned to Cindy. 'Cindy, as you know Gerard has always been a little shy to tell us about his days as a merchant sailor and all those ports and other exotic places he must have visited. So how did you meet Gerard?'

Cindy set her glass of wine slowly down on the table and looked Jean Paul directly in the eye.

'When we were shooting a porn movie,' She answered.

'What?'

'We met on the set of a porn film,' she repeated.

We were all quiet and Jean Paul was clearly in shock.

'Hahaha,' he laughed.

'Gerard was a last minute stand-in and his next sailing wasn't for another week.'

'Gerard?'

'Yes, hasn't he ever told you?'

'No', Jean Paul replied looking over at Gerard, who just shrugged.

'Seriously?'

'Yes, seriously. We had two or three days filming and then we had some fun and then he had to return to his day job.'

Jean Paul continued to bluster.

'You mean Gerard was in a porn movie? This is a joke isn't it? A wind up?'

Cindy shrugged her shoulders and smiled and picked up her glass of wine. Jean Paul still looked shocked and nodded waiting for the joke to unfold. But Cindy did not say anything.

'How on earth did you end up doing that?' Jean Paul asked his friend Gerard.

'I had a friend who I was visiting in between sailings and he was friendly with a guy called Kurt, who was having some health problems and couldn't perform,' Gerard started explaining.

'It's called lack of wood in the business. Poor old Kurt couldn't get it up. So they needed a replacement quickly,' Cindy intervened, 'and the big boy just happened to be at a loose end and after far too many beers one night agreed to give it a go.'

'Like you do,' Gerard laughed.

'Well, you never told me and I never knew.' Jean Paul muttered. He then sat back in his chair and like a light coming on in his head, 'that must mean that you are a porn...I mean actress yourself?'

'Well done Detective' Cindy said.

'I think a round of drinks is in order', I interjected, thinking it was a good moment to loosen the tension.

'You never told me this Gerard. We have known each other since we were at school!', Jean Paul continued to complain.

'I wasn't in the film when we were at school together, Jean Paul. You never asked and I didn't need to tell you. It's not something you boast about and you didn't need to know. I would have regretted it other than for the fact that I met Cindy.'

Cindy looked at us all.

'Let's order some food eh?'

Throughout the evening and the lovely food, cooked by the Scotsman, Randy in the commune sponsored restaurant. Jean Paul kept looking at his friend Gerard and shook his head.

For my part, I did not have a clue as to whether the story Cindy had told about our friend Gerard and herself was true or not. We never did find out that evening nor to this day. It would not surprise me if it was true nor if it was a made up story. As I have related many times before, people's pasts and their tales have not only been refined and altered over time, embellished at times or just told exactly as it happened and memory allows. We all do it to make something funnier, or to sound a better person or even to elicit more sympathy.

Not surprisingly many of us have horrible things that happen and we choose to keep quiet about them or bury them. Even simple sagas or tales or funny jokes that we have been hiding for years, because we simply forget them and suddenly by chance someone says something, or a smell or a song and there it is a long forgotten memory that bursts back into the present.

Was Gerard a temporary porn star? Was Albert Jules really 148 when he died? Did we really live next to a village where a killer poisoned her husband and murdered her lover? Could Jean Paul and Linda really be getting married?

And finally the breeze. What was that breeze that had wafted through our enchanted village? Invisibly, it had meandered through us all and then was suddenly gone. A harmless gentle wind, yet the breeze was to have profound consequences throughout the village, setting off so many events.

Maybe, it was a coincidence, just a harmless set of sequences that were random but they had occurred together. Certainly, on that day La Croix de Bois had appeared to be a healthier place with regards to the pharmacy, where numerous villagers were stopped in their tracks to seek remedies and cures for their ailments that had simply vanished.

Yet the breeze had somehow enabled secrets to be revealed. Secrets hidden for years. Not just secrets but unspoken feelings and yearnings as was the case with Linda and Jean Paul.

The discovery of the stolen Bugatti was to have a very profound impact on several people's lives.

The steins had reunited lost family ties for the Browns and Bruns.

Secrets can remain secrets as long as they are hidden and not sought after. However, by their very nature, secrets lie there waiting to be discovered, dormant but restless to come to the surface. To see the light of day. Secrets burrow their way around one's head and like an animal trap, waiting to be trodden upon and snap, the trap closes and life is never the same again.

Everything changes.

Logic tells me that it must surely just have been a breezy day. Everything that happened was a complete set of unconnected coincidences.

Part of me wishes that was true but I have seen too many things in this village to dismiss such a logical explanation.

Of course, I cannot offer any other theory in its place.

The one thing that I am certain of, is that life in La Croix de Bois is never boring, nor, I would suggest, would it ever be!!!

ABOUT LA CROIX DE BOIS AND ITS INHABITANTS

La Croix de Bois does not exist as a village. It represents a number of fine villages that you will see across Brittany. It has been located in the department of the Cote d'Armor and as a consequence many of the place names around it actually exist as does the history and the folklore, the fables and the superstitions that I have tried to weave in.

The Characters in the books are all 100% fictitious but you cannot move through life without meeting fabulous and bizarre people who leave their mark on you. Whether it is their character, behaviour, or their influences and stories. Such is the richness, it cannot help but spill into the pages of anything that is being written.

Well, that is my excuse and apologies in doing this, if I have offended anyone or anyone's stories in the process.

It has been a privilege meeting so many people over the years and listening to their stories and adventures but for the purposes of these books, there are no friends or foes hidden in these characters, just influences, traits, good thoughts as it should be. I will own up to 'what if this happened?'

As the series has developed, it has been a delight for me to watch some of the characters grow and develop and then to face them with new challenges.

Personally, I would like to live in La Croix de Bois, as it sounds like a great place to live in but I am equally lucky with where I do live and with the people around me. On both counts, you only have to turn the TV, radio or computer on and be confronted with the real world to appreciate where I live and those around me.

THANKYOU

For this story and for the one before it - 'nature abhors a vacuum', I am very grateful to Sandy, who not only corrected my spelling but edited my books to give it both coherence and proper timelines. I admire his forensic ability to do this and the way in which he did this with me.

He had read the first two books and came armed with corrections and observations for them too.

Whilst writing this I also was lucky enough to attend the Jersey Festival of the Word, which was my first ever book festival and public reading. The organisers were brilliant and I saw first hand their professionalism and enthusiasm that always makes it a success – thanks guys.

Once again, there is a beautiful cover painted by my good friend and talented artist Chris Derry.

Garry has demonstrated just how good he is at taking my draft to a design fit for publishing. His humour, his enthusiasm and his skill is always evident in abundance. He is also a very patient man.

So many people and friends have bit parts of the characters in these books and so far I am relieved no one has been upset. All the characters are one hundred percent fictional as are the places but when you are writing the merging of everything in your head makes for creative and happy writing.

Lastly, thank you, to everyone out there, who has recounted a story, or talked of an incident; an insight, or even a joke. Often life throws up things for us all that would seem too far fetched or outlandish to write as fiction. I make no apologies for using them in these books. They are usually too good to leave out.

Until the next time.

Printed by Amazon Italia Logistica S.r.l.
Torrazza Piemonte (TO), Italy